SHERLOCK HOLMES
DISQUIET AT ALBANY

In one of his most disturbing cases yet, Sherlock Holmes is called to the prestigious Albany in Piccadilly, a residence for wealthy bachelors, to investigate the disappearance of Ethby Sands and his valet. When nothing appears untoward, Holmes and Watson depart to investigate a murder in Norfolk. Holmes is confident in his ability to solve the crime, but when a second murder takes place, just as grisly as the first, and it becomes clear that the missing man may be connected to the atrocities, a far more sinister web of intrigue begins to emerge that will test Sherlock to the very limits of his powers.

SHERLOCK HOLMES
DISQUIET AT ALBANY

Sherlock Holmes Disquiet At Albany

Published by arrangement with the estate
of the late Doctor Watson, M.D.

by

N. M. Scott

Magna Large Print Books
Long Preston, North Yorkshire,
BD23 4ND, England.

British Library Cataloguing in Publication Data.

Scott, N. M.
    Sherlock Holmes disquiet at Albany.

    A catalogue record of this book is
    available from the British Library

    ISBN   978-0-7505-4214-2

First published in Great Britain in 2014 by The Book Guild Ltd.

Copyright © N. M. Scott 2014

Cover illustration by arrangement with Book Guild Publishing

The right of N. M. Scott to be identified as the author of this work has been asserted by him in accordance with the Copyright, Designs and Patents Act, 1988.

Published in Large Print 2016 by arrangement with
Book Guild Publishing

Magna Large Print is an imprint of Library Magna Books Ltd.

Printed and bound in Great Britain by
T.J. (International) Ltd., Cornwall, PL28 8RW

*Especially for Aunt Marie, Aunt Heather
and Aunt Janet (and Frank, Phil and Clive).
Also for Pauline and Mariette,
Dot Dodswell and Keith
and Cynthia Gogel and Joanna Walder.*

Acknowledgements

Grateful thanks to all at Book Guild Publishing and, as always, Amanda Payne, Olivia Guest, and the staff at my local library.

The characters created by Sir Arthur Conan Doyle are used here by kind permission of Jonathan Clowes Ltd, on behalf of Andrea Plunket, administrator of the Conan Doyle copyrights.

Contents

Contents

1

The Porter Knocks Twice

I confess I am surprised at my industry, and shall allow myself the satisfaction of writing a very brief account of a case which I had fairly copied out in my notebooks, and still possess, but which, due to the laws of criminal libel governing usage of names of persons still living, has remained until now extinct from the public domain. My colleague, Mr Sherlock Holmes's love of the science of deduction is well known – the process by which he could, even from a very brief abstract theory, solve the most puzzling of crimes, a science that gradually predominated over every other taste. How great was his joy when a solution occurred to him – how despondent and low when there occurred a period of inactivity, and, alas, there was no case available to solve.

Anyhow, I am about to embark upon a brief sketch of my dear friend, whom I have known better than any other and with whom over the years I enjoyed the privilege of sharing digs, accompanying him on adventures and recording his many and varied cases for posterity.

Upon the morning of a gusty autumnal day at the end of October, following a night of stormy gales that had caused structural damage and blown slates off the roofs of the houses opposite, I heard a couple of knocks upon the door, and a personage entirely unknown to us, penitently standing with bowler hat in hand, appeared at our rooms in Baker Street. He was a big man, with a square Teutonic head that could have been carved from a block of granite, a large-boned and heavy-set jaw, and dressed very smartly. He had clipped hair and side-whiskers, a long-tailed jacket and stiff, starched white collar turned down at the edges. He hesitated upon the threshold until at length was moved to say, 'Shadwell, Lew Shadwell. I 'opes I h'aint interrupting, gents.'

Holmes smiled in an assenting manner. 'Come in dear fellow, come in. Don't stand there out on the landing. You are a concierge, else a porter, at Albany I perceive, for although you've dispensed with your smart uniform top hat and coat, you persist in wearing a pair of the most distinctive maroon trousers in the West End. The sharply defined emerald green stripe down the side is the giveaway.'

My colleague bent forward and agitated the flames of the somewhat subdued sea-coal fire with the poker, waving away intrusive smoke being blown down the chimney by the wind presently howling along Baker Street.

'Mr Shadwell, that's it. Here, have a cigarette, draw a chair up to the hearth. Watson, be a good fellow and pour our breakfast visitor a cup of coffee. My, my, this wretched smoking chimney is a bind.'

'I wondered if I might 'ave a word, Mr Holmes. I am, as you correctly infer, a porter at Albany. I must emphasise our code is strictly no publicity, so we must needs be discreet.'

'Perfectly proper,' Holmes rejoined.

'Well sir, a gentleman what lives in an apartment upstairs, or "set" as they are referred to by us porters and residents alike, a Mister Ethby Sands, has not been seen or heard of for a fortnight. I took the liberty of opening his rooms this morning and, with your permission, I shall relate certain disturbing details.'

'By all means Mister Shadwell. I recall, Watson, Ethby Sands was once an M.P., chairman of the Conservative Party and an eminent Justice of the Peace, who sadly was forced to resign his constituency due to ill health. He inherited a good deal of money from his father's agricultural machinery business and owns what is judged the finest collection of stuffed red birds of paradise in the country.'

'Yes, I read in *The Times*,' said I, 'that he, along with the Marquis of Anglesey, helped sponsor the explorer and naturalist Alfred Russell Wallace on his voyage to the Indonesian spice islands, or Moluccas as they are called. Wallace generally financed his work by sending rare zoological specimens to an agent in London who sold them on to museums or wealthy collectors such as Mr Sands. He spent much of his time in the western part of Indonesia visiting Sumatra, Java, Borneo and Sarawak. That was between '54 and '56 I believe.'

'Oh, them bootiful stuffed red birds of paradise are a feature of 'is set sir. Keeps 'em in lovely glass-fronted display cabinets, does Mr Sands.

But I diversify. If I may continue, with my first impressions of Mr Sands's set, unusually his wheeled chair, such a part of him since he became gravely ill, was stuck at angles in the hall, the rug being slung in a most slovenly way across the arm-rests, not like his valet Garson would approve of, Mr Holmes, so that's something out of character. Next, I dare to say this sir, I noticed what looked to be like bloodstains upon the Turkey hearth rug before the mantelpiece. Additionally, a crumpled up bundle of newspaper in the wicker waste basket by his escritoire looked to me to be also stained with blood.'

'Might I congratulate you, Mr Shadwell. You are first rate in your observations of minutiae – a "natural". Pray, enlighten us further. For instance, were the valet's bowler and winter overcoat absent from the hall stand?'

'Well, that's the crunch, there's just no sign of Mr Garson the valet – or of his master. The set looked to be abandoned at short notice – coffee cups unwashed, beds unmade, but it's that bloomin' blood what worries me most, gentlemen. The rules at Albany is no dogs, no children, no silly noise – and I have to be absolutely clear here, Mr Holmes, *no publicity of any kind*. My residents, some of whom are crown princes, members of the aristocracy, talented artists and musicians, top milliners, actors of distinction, would definitely frown upon their privacy being invaded by any pushy policemen nosing around disturbing the refined atmosphere. I mean, Albany is exclusive, wonderfully situ'hated in Piccadilly. We don't want no coppers, thank you very much. I mean, certainly Mr Sands's absence bothers me, but not to the point of wishing to contact the official force and risk offending residents.'

'Discretion is assured, Mr Shadwell, and we can of course entirely rule out Scotland Yard. From what you have so far told me in confidence, you obviously fear Mr Sands may have been criminally abducted.'

'What else am I to make of it? Mr Sands is a most gregarious and engaging individual. He, or at least Mr Garson, should never dream of absconding like this, going off somewhere without h'informing us porters. Why Mr Holmes, he has been a resident at Albany for more years than I care to remember. We are on most pleasant and convivial terms. I pride meself on being a trusted confidante of personages, famous or otherwise, who live in our exclusive apartment block.'

'Quite so, quite proper. I comprehend the delicate situation this places you under. One further point, Shadwell – you are certain in consulting with colleagues that Ethby Sands and his valet Mr Garson on no account left Albany by the front entrance or via the Rope Walk in the past fortnight?'

'Positive – but that's just it, you see, Mr Sands has been ill for some time, suffering from a wasting disease that has left him very weak and reliant on his valet for everything. He would be incapable of walking anywhere, even if he wanted to. He has been confined to a wheeled chair for the past six months or so, so you can understand, gentlemen, why I am so worried.'

2

The Collector of Stuffed Birds of Paradise

Allowing Mr Shadwell to make his own way on the subterranean railway, our clothes flapping and holding onto our hats for dear life, we hailed a hansom outside our diggings and, with a persistent sharp wind in evidence, it being very cold in London where there had been a flourish of sleety rain the previous day, our cab was soon rattling down Old Bond Street, my companion wholly concerned with checking his leather pocketbook, for it turned out we had an appointment at Fortnum & Mason's restaurant to share a pot of tea and cakes at the invitation of our theatre friends, the impresario Langton Lovell and his business partner, Charles Lemon, the acclaimed actor. A dazzling new musical, a light opera, was on the horizon and they were anxious we should meet both the composer and lyricist responsible for writing the new production, which would be having its opening night at the Wimborne Theatre in Drury Lane the following week. We occasionally dined with Lovell and Lemon at Goldini's, else Simpson's-in-the-Strand, and had known them for a number of years.

Albany, that most stately of Georgian piles, situated so conveniently in the heart of Piccadilly, a stone's throw from the grandeur of St James, is a bastion of privacy. The inhabitants guard the tenure of their selective sets with alacrity.

'My brother Mycroft lived here for a time,' remarked Holmes, faintly smiling, putting his pocketbook away as our cab drew up outside the main entrance.

'Did he indeed?' said I, surprised by my friend's revelation concerning his portly brother.

'The exclusivity, the monastic bachelor ambience, the nearness of Fortnum's, Burlington Arcade, within walking distance of St James or the Houses of Westminster – all this appealed to him wonderfully. My dear Watson, surely it is no secret that the "picky" board of trustees who oversee this establishment show favouritism towards members of the Diogenes Club above all others when a set becomes vacant for occupancy. Ah, Mr Shadwell, lead the way.'

After we had been shown the Rope Walk, we hurried through the main entrance with its imposing pedimented façade, then along the central corridor adorned with busts, including a fine representation of Lord Byron, to a staircase whither was situated the set in which Ethby Sands resided, or at least should have resided.

'Last summer, Mr Holmes, you always saw Mr Sands in that little ivy-clad garden we saw earlier, sunning himself by the bronze statue of Antonius at the Fountain. It was his own little space. Mr Garson was always so attentive to his master and would keep him amused with observances of life going on in and around Piccadilly when out shopping.'

'Most commendable. Could you let us in Mr

Shadwell?' Holmes asked. 'Time is moving along, you know.'

'Forgive my rambling on so, let me just put the key in.'

With the door open, it was surely that abandoned wheeled chair with the untidy rug thrown over it that seemed to admonish our intrusion, looking at us accusingly as if to imply 'he who it was sat on me once was murdered'. But Holmes paid little heed, bounding into the airy, tastefully furnished sitting room. There was a Chinese Chippendale chair, a linen Chesterfield sofa. Ming porcelain vases sat either side of the marble mantelpiece, and a gilt-framed portrait of Ethby Sands in the House of Commons hung above. In plain words, it was a bachelor's nest, comfortable and unfussy, books and a box of Coronas to hand, a japanned upright piano which I pointed out to Holmes standing in the bay, and of course a collection of stuffed red birds of paradise beautifully displayed behind glass and extending into many of the other rooms in the apartment.

'A remarkable collection,' I conceded, forgetting for a time that we were visiting Albany for a purpose.

'And lo! There, gentlemen, is the bloody stain. The hearth rug shall require a good soaking in a solution of soft soap to shift it.'

'Step aside Mr Shadwell, I shall not be long.'

Brandishing his magnifying lens, upon an impulse of curiosity my colleague got down on his knees, his great beak of a nose almost touching the floor.

'Gawd 'elp us, it 'as to be murder, don't it,

Doctor Watson?' said the house porter grimly.

Holmes made a slight grimace. 'I believe I can offer a simpler alternative, my dear Shadwell,' he said, springing up on his feet once more. 'For I can detect scuff marks in the ropey fibres of the Turkey rug, but not blood.'

'What then?'

'Cherry Blossom shoe polish of a rich, red tint. Likewise I have already checked the crumpled pages of a London *Daily Echo* extracted from the waste paper basket.'

'And...'

Holmes broke into a light laugh. 'Smudged with boot polish.'

'Well I'm blowed,' the porter exclaimed.

'It is a simple enough deduction. I perceive an over-vigorous use of the shoe brush responsible, a sheet of newspaper not placed in proper alignment. Ethby Sands does wear a pair of red shoes presumably?'

The porter hurried out into the hall to check. 'I last saw a pair of red loafers out here, Mr Holmes.'

'He must be wearing them.'

'But what use would they be to him, sir? He cannot walk. Like I says, he's stuck in a wheeled chair. Of late his feet swelled up so bad 'e wore carpet slippers with the toes slit like a turtle's mouth.'

'A conundrum of footwear,' chuckled my companion. 'Now, Mr Shadwell, we do have a pressing engagement at Fortnum's tea rooms. You have already established that the valet's bowler and winter overcoat are absent from the hall stand, as are Mr Sands's gentleman's hat and coat – and scarf. Now, consider this carefully: did the ex-MP have a favourite walking stick, an ivory-handled cane, for instance?'

'Good 'eavens, Mr Holmes, now you come to mention it, he used always to favour a metal-headed walking stick bearing a silver, hallmarked ferrule. Would not be seen without it when out strolling along Piccadilly.'

'But it is missing. A group of bamboo handled umbrellas is all I see in the stand.'

'Yes, it's gone sir. Lor', I 'ope I haven't wasted your time gentlemen,' said he, a little put out. 'That bloomin' blood – boot polish, I ask you. I should have been more thorough, checking my facts first before comin' round to Baker Street.'

'On the contrary, you were most wise to alert me to the possibility of some criminal enterprise and I congratulate you for it, Shadwell. I shall keep all this in mind, and do not fail to contact me again if Mr Sands fails to return to his set in the next few days. Now Watson, onwards to Fortnum's.'

3

Tea at Fortnum's

The blustery weather did not abate, with rain expected later. Holding onto our hats we crossed the main road, then a brisk walk under steely-grey, overcast skies brought us to the famous emporium at No. 181 Piccadilly. Passing through the opulent food hall, upstairs we found a delighted Langton Lovell and Charles Lemon frantically beckoning us over to a table set for six persons. A waitress busied herself arranging the tea things.

Two people whom I did not recognise, one who had his face buried in a musical score, the other charming and amiable, a cheerier personality altogether, were introduced to us as the lyricist Philip Troy and composer Christopher Chymes respectively, both working on the new musical and even now putting finishing touches to the score. In fact, they would be going on to a full dress rehearsal later, it being less than a fortnight before the light opera was to be performed for the first time in front of an invited audience of guests and West End theatre critics at the Wimborne Theatre. All concerned hoped it would become a smash box office hit. During casual conversation I learnt that Christopher Chymes was himself a resident at Albany, staying temporarily at the exclusive block of apartments because his father, when not abroad in Morocco, lived there.

'Yes, I know Ethby to nod to. I mean, none of us gets involved with small talk. We're all fairly reserved and respect each other's privacy when at home, but I have occasionally bumped into him along the Rope Walk. Garson, his valet, is a gentleman's gentleman and a first-rate fellow. If I'm out shopping along the arcade he'll invariably doff his bowler and stop for a chat. It's so damned appalling that Ethby, now confined to a wheeled chair, hardly ever emerges from his set.

Old Garson told me in confidence the doctors have given up on him. They give him a month at most. Such a pity his parliamentary career got cut short like that just because of that wasting disease. A human skeleton, "rag bag of bones" is how he describes his master when out shopping in Piccadilly. Damned shame.

'Of course, I'm busy at my piano writing tunes all day, preparing the score. I want to hear that overture stomp, stomp, stomp, and deliver such a catchy melody that all the audience will be up on their feet and clapping their hands in under fifty seconds flat. Philip's written some amazing lyrics. He looks rather a miserable chap, but he writes the sweetest phrases, and of course when Langton and Charles read the music and words they immediately took us under their wing and we haven't looked back since.'

'Yes, I'm sure show business is tough to break into,' I conceded.

'Ethby Sands – wasn't he a Tory M.P. or something?' mumbled Philip Troy, uttering only a brief pronouncement before disappearing behind his sheaves of script once more.

'Oh, and another thing, Doctor Watson. I did on one occasion get to see his collection of stuffed birds. He told me how Alfred Wallace managed to trap and kill them in Indonesia. The natives are apparently very partial to the colourful feathers, too. Poor old birds of paradise, that's what I say. I mean, I doubt if there can be many left, can there?'

Of the pair I judged Chymes the more outward going, intensely charming, handsome and debonair, suited and booted by the finest Savile

Row tailor and Lobb for footwear. He wore an expensive men's fragrance. I should have hit on 'Floris' or 'Trumpers of Bond Street'. The fellow was a pleasure to share tea and conversation with.

Philip Troy, however, was silent and morose. He appeared to me permanently buttoned up and unresponsive to jovial banter, preferring to sit and occasionally sip his tea, scowling at his pocket watch else examining that dratted score, anxious to get away to the theatre, I should imagine, and see the first run-through, check out how the chorus sounded, so I supposed I shouldn't be too hard on the fellow. This was their first big break and I think he was nervous and on edge because of it.

Anyhow, promising Lovell and Lemon we would be there at the Wimborne on the big night, of course we would, and assuring them we wished them every success with their new musical, we bid everyone adieu.

4

Return to Baker Street

After bidding our theatre friends good day, we headed downstairs to Fortnum's food hall on the ground floor, which stocked a wide range of luxury goods. At the counter we purchased packets of exotic tea, 'Gentlemen's Relish' and potted meats for ourselves, and a boar's head in aspic jelly as a special treat for Mrs Hudson, who of late had been showing signs of disapproval after complaining about Holmes's late-night chemistry, particularly the foul odour upon the stairs and upstairs landing that for some reason had lingered for days without dispersing. My profuse apologies to our landlady on behalf of my wilful colleague had met with angry stares and I noted our normally first-rate breakfasts and suppers of late often arrived cold, else under-cooked, a broad hint that some mode of reparation was in order.

'Watson, do you perchance recall last Wednesday's edition of the *Telegraph?*'

'The rugby scores, certainly,' said I.

'A Norfolk murder – it got barely a mention?' Holmes enquired as our cab rattled round the Circus.

'Quite possibly.' I now recalled the short but succinct article on page fourteen headlined *'Grizzly death. Eel catcher horribly mutilated on the Broads, Norwich police baffled.'*

'Now I remember – you commented on it at the time.'

'I received a letter this morning from Inspector Wells of the Norfolk force, requesting in the gravest of terms that I should become involved in a consulting capacity. Incidentally, Watson, the official police surgeon, who remembers you from when you were studying at St Bartholomew's Hospital, insisted I be contacted, for the Norfolk murder bears all the exquisite hallmarks of a classic case, in which my peculiarly unique skills can be tested to the extreme.'

'You sound like a blasted antiques dealer, Holmes, crowing about a fine piece of rare Ming porcelain picked up at some house sale. A human being is involved who has family, remember.'

'Be that as it may, we pack for Norfolk this evening, Watson, and leave early tomorrow morning. Your service revolver will of course be requisite for such an excursion into the wetland regions, the damp and dreary climes of the Broads. Let us hope Mrs Hudson shall not serve up yet another inedible supper. Still, I think our handsome pig's head in jelly shall go some way to appeasing our redoubtable Scotch landlady.'

5

Train to Norfolk

According to our well-thumbed copy of *Bradshaw's Guide*, we were to travel upon the North London Railway before joining the Great Eastern main line which would take us into the county of Norfolk, thence at Norwich we would change trains for a stopping service up the branch to Great Melchett Halt, whence the train continued up the single line to Cromer, that coastal resort renowned for its sea bathing.

A calmer, less blowy morning found us plumped upon cloth-covered seats lounging in a first-class smoker of the Norfolk Express, replete with a bundle of newspapers to help while away the long journey, plus a 2/6d lunch basket for refreshment.

'Time is of the essence,' said Holmes, crossing his long legs and searching for his pipe and matches, sulphurous smoke from the locomotive in front wafting past our compartment window as we departed King's Cross and headed for the provinces. The morning was cloudy and overcast, a fine shower of rain splashing the glass as our train gathered speed and rumbled over points, passing beneath the gantry of signals.

'What of Ethby Sands, the missing chap from Albany? Does the case interest you sufficiently or is it a dud? That porter, is he worrying unnecessarily, making a fuss, a mountain out of a molehill? The theatre crowd didn't seem too bothered, after all.'

'I grant you, the possibility of Sands being forcibly removed from his set appears slim, but that deuced wheeled chair left in the hall poses a conundrum. How can a fellow who is supposedly gravely ill with not much time to live and without the use of his legs simply get up one morning and walk out of the door, his valet by his side and neither of them be heard of or seen for a fortnight? No, we cannot rule out foul play altogether. And then there's the queer matter of that missing walking stick.'

'The what?'

'The singular metal-headed walking stick, his favourite – absent from the hall stand.'

'Perhaps the blighter's bluffing, making out he's an invalid when in fact he's as fit as a fiddle, in perfect health – some insurance scam. It does happen, Holmes.'

'Of course, that is a possibility, Watson. If however it turns out he was abducted from his set under duress, I shall of course intervene. Have you a vesta handy, old man? I appear to have mislaid my matches.'

Travelling express upon Eastern main line metals, by mid-afternoon we had achieved Norwich in good time to change trains for the Cromer push-pull service, which departed in ten minutes.

'Ah, do you smell the pondweed tang of the wetlands, Watson? The Broads are not far off, our journey's end is in sight.'

'What a wet and miserable day,' I commented, gazing forlornly out of the window of our stationary passenger coach, considering vaguely the old castle upon the hill, and a light engine earning its keep shunting eight or so trucks laden with sugar beet and a rake of empty parcels vans into a siding. Whilst I pondered the gas works, a manure siding, timber stacked in a yard, our compartment door was pulled open with a bang. Our guard, frowning in a most officious manner, held onto a form which he passed inside to us.

'Another murder. I have been requested by our station master at Norwich, Mr Eades, to deliver this urgent telegraph message sent down the wires from Great Melchett signal box. You are the Mr Sherlock Holmes referred to here, I take it?'

'Here's a florin for your trouble, guard. A return message, take this down, inform your telegraph office to send the following reply: "Inspector Wells, be with you on the one o'clock cross country

31

service from Norwich, arrives at Great Melchett Halt 1.35 p.m. Require horse and trap. Sherlock Holmes."'

The guard duly wrote down all Holmes had related with the stub of his pencil and without delay, for we had but five minutes left until departure, rushed off down the platform.

'A second murder, Holmes. What does this Inspector Wells have to say?'

'Bears all the similarities of the first murder. By Jove, Watson, it appears the killer has struck twice in the last fortnight. A grizzly murder too! Perfect for occupying one's mind on a penetratingly cold and damp afternoon, don't you agree?'

Our little two-coach train departed Norwich on time and proceeded to bustle up the branch northward towards Cromer. As our engine blew off steam, our carriages rattling over points, it dawned on me that we were quite possibly the only passengers on the train.

Holmes was positively straining at the leash and couldn't wait to apply his clever brain to the case at hand. At length we drew into our station, just a basic waiting room and parcels office supporting a pagoda shelter.

Barely had we a chance to grab our luggage and walking sticks from the rack above, when there was a loud rap on the pane of the compartment window and we saw a great strapping chap with a florid complexion, wearing a soft cloth cap and plus-fours, about to open the door for us. This just had to be our Inspector Wells, of the Norfolk Constabulary. He helped us down. A little further along the platform, we encountered a dug-up flower bed edged in clay bricks, the name of the station displayed in whitewashed stones against the backdrop of the station master's runner-bean sticks. Beyond the end of the platform were a pair of level crossing gates and a fellow working the signals in his box. A porter, who barely registered our arrival, was stacking milk churns atop a trolley. The grey, lowering sky, the constant drizzly rain damping everything in sight, somehow offered a portent. This was no holiday jaunt but a serious matter of murder and I was impressed by the officious but polite way in which the detective welcomed us to this region of the Broads.

'Glad to meet you, I'm sure. Inspector Wells, up from Norwich. This is a grim business, gentlemen. It is a vile crime and I must warn you the body discovered but a few hours previous by a local wildfowler is in pieces and being reassembled as we speak.'

6

Murder on the Broads

In no time we were rattling along in a horse and trap, being taken to the scene of the most recent murder at a lonely place on the Broads called Potters Ditch, where there was apparently a derelict windmill, long neglected and allowed to deteriorate, overlooking the channel.

'Walpole St Thomas lies that way, gentlemen,'

explained Wells. 'The hamlet of Great Melchett is beyond the trees on the far side of that field of swede and turnip, and the road we are travelling on leads eventually to Cromer. Unfortunately I hear the North Sea is claiming the resort for its own and the cliffs are crumbling away.'

To our right was the unending expanse of wetlands and reed beds that formed the famous Broads. All right in summer with the sail boats and holiday tourists, but this gloomy October afternoon the chilly dampness seeped right into one's bones.

'It's a determined fellow who poaches on these marshes of a misty evening,' remarked Wells.

'Indeed, what is there to interest the eye?' I remarked. 'The odd, deformed, windswept hedgerow tree, labourers' cottages dotted about. I have seldom seen a lonelier and more desolate terrain.' I felt the dampness settle on my clothes, my face cold and wet from the ever persistent autumnal drizzle which had not let up since our arrival at the station halt.

'The victim was using a coracle, you say, inspector?' enquired Holmes. 'The shallow punt should have been more my preference.'

'Ideal for stalking duck and other wildfowl for the pot. But this chap were checking his baskets at the time and it was during his inspection for eels that the ferocious attack occurred. Ah, we've almost reached the windmill at Potters Ditch. The sails, you will observe, were long ago dismantled. The place is in a sorry state of repair. There is now a pumping station further up and the mill fell out of use long ago.'

Once we had jumped down from the trap and the horse had been tethered and fed his hay, we ambled across to the edge of a wide channel. A small island lay in the middle of gently lapping water, dark green and silted up due to the to-ing and fro-ing of the police officers in a row boat being ferried across to the island by a local wild-fowler who was familiar with the area.

'The injuries are wholly consistent with a violent, swift attack by a person of great physical prowess who would have been a clever swimmer,' explained Wells. 'The tidal flow is strong below the water. Misleading, as the channel appears calm, with the surface of the water barely disturbed.'

The police surgeon in attendance, whom I vaguely recognised from my time at St Bartholomew's Hospital as a fellow student, but whose name I could not for the life of me recall, came over and shook hands.

'Watson, isn't it?' he said, staring at me so I became a trifle uncomfortable. 'Clayborne, Timothy Clayborne.'

'Oh yes, I think you were in my year. This is Mr Sherlock Holmes.'

'Glad to meet you, sir. This is a difficult case to crack. Only last week I was up here, a little further along the channel where the remains of a headless body were found on the bank amongst the patches of rushes. The injuries were severe. Do you want to share my flask of brandy? I can see our climate up here in Norfolk doesn't suit either of you metropolitans. In the autumn we do get a lot of rain and mist. How are you bearing up, Watson? Like me, looking forward to a good dinner and a warming fire to dry out, I should wager.'

'The pull of the convivial old country inn is very strong,' I laughed. 'Yes, I'm ravenous. Can you recommend a hostelry in Great Melchett where we can get a bed and board for the night, Clayborne?'

'The Duck and Drake is a warm and hospitable inn. They offer bed and breakfast and can knock you up a good meal at short notice. Isaiah Hooper is the landlord.'

Calm as anything, Clayborne drew back a blanket of old sacking and Holmes and myself were confronted with a body much mutilated and torn about. My training as a doctor saw me in good stead, for a strong stomach is required on such occasions. The torso bore a distinctive tattoo – a "hawk in flight" – across the broad chest which offered the best likelihood of identifying the victim, we surmised.

'The body parts were found where exactly, inspector?' asked Holmes, inquisitively.

The detective, wearing his gum boots, indicated to the island in the middle of the channel, as if floating in reeds. 'A local wildfowler by the name of Hobtree, lurking hereabouts with his punt and gun, often uses the island as a useful vantage for bagging ducks. Upon scrambling up the bank partly concealed by rushes, he came across the remains. He is a local man and by the distinctive tattoo on the torso realised at once the body belonged to his compatriot Frank Peters, who is often at this time of year to be found eel-catching, setting up his baskets and periodically checking the contents, else baiting the pots.'

'Capital! Observe, Watson, the overturned coracle clogged in the shallows. The island, you say – so the poor fellow was tipped out of the coracle and dragged across the space of water into the reeds. That would certainly require a strong swimmer.'

'A swimmer of unique muscular character- istics, sir. The current is very strong – deceptively so.'

'The channel must have been fearfully cold at this time of year?'

'Yes, a hardy swimmer, someone who managed to get that body – *for the victim was not a small man either, of light stature but well built and weighing in at I should say fourteen stone* – across the stretch of water, up the bank and, in what must surely have been an unstoppable frenzy, killed Peters and fled the scene.'

'By a punt or a coracle, I wonder? A row boat? The first Norfolk murder, if my memory serves me correctly, and I am recalling its geographical location from an article that appeared in last Thursday's edition of the *Telegraph*, occurred further along the bank where there exists a reed-thatched barn, more towards Dunham St Paul.'

'That is correct. The headless body of George Flemps was found close by. But still we cannot fathom the physical nature of the perpetrator of that heinous crime.'

'You infer an animal of some kind. Come now, Inspector Wells, we are in East Anglia – not the plains of Africa. No man-eating tigers or leopards in this neck of the woods. Nor is there, according

37

to my pocket map, which I minutely consulted on our journey up here from King's Cross, any private sanctuary or public zoo in the vicinity of the Broads. Pray, what creature could have been large enough to inflict such injuries – a water rat, a vole, a mink! That really is a tiresome supposition. Might I venture to confirm – we are looking for a frenzied madman, a lunatic, someone driven by an abiding hatred for humanity. You know, such people do exist, Wells, and it is our job to hunt them down. I should like to amble across to the windmill and examine the location. Watson, be a good fellow and retrieve my tape measure and tweezers from your bag, old man. Still pining for a good dinner? Well, we shall soon be done with our sleuth-hounding for the day. The light is starting to fade anyhow. See, the constables are gathering up poor Peters' remains on a stretcher. Clayborne, I see you're finished with the corpse for now and must be damned anxious to make an autopsy at Walpole St Thomas where the inquiry is based. Would you care to accompany us across to the windmill while there is still light?'

'I should be honoured, Mr Holmes. Your being here in Norfolk has certainly livened up the local force no end. My own findings at present would concur with your lunatic theory. Who else could, with such physical strength and determination, swim across a strong current, dragging a body through the water during a particularly wet autumn which has seen severe flooding in these parts?'

'Just so. Now we shall make a closer inspection of the building. Your brandy flask, Clayborne, I have need of fire in my belly for I'm chilled to the bone. My clothes are soaked through. A tipple for each of us is prerequisite to our foray across to that old windmill. Hello! What's this?' My colleague's hawk-like features broke into a scowl. 'Watson, you know my methods. Pray, what do you discern upon the path?'

'Holes, like the stumps of a wicket would make.'

'The marks of a walking stick, old fellow, the ferrule embedded quite deeply in the giving ground of Potters Ditch – evenly spaced. Clayborne, I observed no police activity in this area. The muddy path is relatively undisturbed, is it not?'

'Agreed. I noticed the police sergeant wander over here earlier but he possessed no staff or stout walking stick, or cane to lean on.'

'Traces of the ferrule's point appear to lead from the direction of the windmill and all of a sudden cease. Of course, a harmless rambler cannot be ruled out. No signs of the paw marks of a dog in tow though. We shall stroll across to that windmill, then it's dinner and early to bed at the Duck and Drake.'

The mill was not of a wooden post construction, but rather a tapering brick tower with a tiny framed window uppermost. Holmes's keen eye settled on the entrance door which had recently been defaced. The rain was falling hard and causing the ground to become even more muddy and waterlogged.

'This graffiti is recent. Observe the way in which the wood has been whittled away by the blade of a sharp penknife, the impromptu carving exposing the lighter grain beneath. It purports to show the image of a large rodent. A penknife or chisel has been diligently employed, and the artistry is really quite clever. What say you, Watson?'

'I am in full agreement, Holmes,' said I. 'This is no mere childish scratching by a bored youth.'

Inspector Wells, after supervising the removal of the body to a farm wagon for transportation to the village hall at Walpole St Thomas, had come over to join us.

'A rat. You know, gentlemen, there has been a spate of graffiti recently. The last week or so "Ratty" has been appearing everywhere, from telegraph poles to front doors to defaced head-stones. The local constable is being inundated with complaints, but no one is able to apprehend the rascal because this unconventional artist comes "as a thief in the night", as the Good Book says.'

'Be that as it may, Inspector Wells, I believe you should be aware that our murderer is possibly someone who uses a thin walking stick with a half-inch diameter ferrule. The marks appear to spread out along the path, leading away from the windmill, ceasing abruptly some ten yards or so distant from the edge of the reed bank.'

7

A Room at the Inn

Clambering over the five-barred gate across the lane, we trudged with difficulty across a claggy, arable field of root crops, trusting to link with a footpath that led eventually through a group of trees to the hamlet of Great Melchett. The stack of the old sail-less windmill beside the waterway was now a dark silhouette on the low horizon. As evening fell, I heard a locomotive whistle and was reminded of our two-coach train from Norwich from which we had alighted, and the little halt with its crossing gates and box a mile or so distant.

'I must say, Holmes, the fatty tissue of the thigh appeared to me to have been gnawed to the bone. The victim's stomach was clawed open, leaving the intestines exposed.'

'Ah, we are onto anatomy, eh? Well, old man, the throat was clean ripped out,' Holmes declared as we turned onto our footpath.

'See the old manor house at the end of the lane? Fifteenth century, I'll wager. It has gabled windows and pedimented stone arches. I wonder who owns such a place. There's a walled kitchen garden and various grades of glass house visible.'

We ordered our beer and boiled mutton in the snug of the Duck and Drake, a most charming country inn with a low timbered ceiling, brownish yellow walls well seasoned by generations of smokers, heavy oak furniture, horse brasses and a homely log fire crackling in the settle of an enormous stone fireplace. We commented on the old manor and it turned out that Foxbury Hall, the property of Lord Astor, was, for the winter months, from September to March, rented out to, of all people, Ethby Sands, who before his illness had been M.P. for Norwich. Nothing had been seen of him. The valet Garson was more sociable, particularly with the ladies, but this season nothing much had been seen of him either. A landau was parked out front on the gravel drive and remained unused.

'Mr Sands is very ill, gentlemen,' said the landlord. 'I've heard reports he is nearing the end and has not long to live. He weakens daily. I believe our local builder is preparing a coffin. That'll be twopence apiece for the beer and fourpence halfpenny for the dinner. Thankee kindly, gents.'

'Thank you landlord. Have you any tobacco, perchance? A strong mixture?'

'Help yourself from the jar, sir. Do you require a clay churchwarden? The tobacco is on the house.'

'My charred old briar will be adequate for my needs, thank you landlord, but I think another pint of your excellent "Old Worthy" is in order.'

We were about to return to the snug to enjoy our ale, smoke our pipes and take stock of events, when a clergyman looking most perplexed and out of sorts wandered into the hostelry. 'Dear me,' he snorted, 'I fear this wretched unknown artist who holds the rodent population in such high esteem has struck again!'

'Aye,' said the landlord, wiping a pewter tankard behind the bar. 'I 'ears Miss Morley the spinster at Crystal Cottage reported her front door had been defaced, besmirched by black paint. Some-one unseen and unknown, the culprit.'

'How long must this sorry state of affairs con-tinue? Another murder I hear over at Potters Ditch and we have barely buried the first victim, poor George Flemps. It just won't do. To be decapitated like that.'

'Was the head ever found, vicar? They dredged the channel using nets the week afore last.'

'No, Isiah, but dear me, please spare the grue-some details. I see we have two gentlemen pre-sent.'

'Please sit down, padre,' said Holmes kindly, striking a vesta to light his pipe. 'Might I order you a glass of sherry, or something stronger? A cherry brandy? The air is so damp and chill at this time of day.'

'Most kind. I am the incumbent here, the Rev. Marsden-Lee. I shall have a cherry brandy if you don't mind. Oh dear me, this wretched outbreak of graffiti in our Christian, law-abiding commun-ity has left me quite irritable and put out. Still, these things are sent to test one's faith, I sup-pose.'

'Perhaps I could be of assistance,' said Holmes, surrounded by a blue-tinged wreath of tobacco smoke. 'I have some small experience concerning the dealings of petty crime.' He chuckled, nudg-ing me in the ribs as I drank the dregs of my Old

Worthy. 'I'm quite the puzzle-solver, you know.'

'Well, I would be glad of some help, sir. It concerns the wall of my vestry.'

8

A Puzzle of Graffiti

'Your marshland church is "decorated and perpendicular" – late medieval I should wager,' remarked Holmes as we crossed to the churchyard and passed beneath the venerable old lychgate.

'Oh, indeed, we are fortunate enough to possess a much later painted window of thirty-four panels, its original glass preserved.'

We traipsed round the side of the church by means of a path, and were thereafter presented with a round-headed arch above an old oak door, weather-worn by centuries of lashing rain and mists seeping off the marsh of waterways and islands known as The Broads. Not long after, we were stood in the vestry over by a cupboard where they kept surplices, appraising a caricature of a large rat boldly painted on the room's whitewashed wall.

'I am at a loss where to begin,' exclaimed the clergyman.

'A puzzle easily enough solved. The mystery is already partly cleared up, at least,' said my colleague with a bored air.

'Solved? You mean you have some idea who is

actually responsible? Gentlemen, I am witness to a miracle. Pray, what on earth has prompted you to declare so easy a victory?'

'Here on the stone paving, padre, and over there by the left of your desk – ah, and also beneath the encased vestry window, lie the dog-ends of cigarettes. It may interest you to know I have written a small monograph concerning one hundred and forty known varieties of tobacco. The ash I refer to. We are presently looking for a person addicted to hand-rolled cigarettes.'

'Yes, I'm with you.'

'Liquorice paper – so distinctive.'

'Indeed, brown is the colour.'

'Cork filters. Mark you, slightly stained with blood. Our quicksilver artist suffers from a chaffed, prominent upper lip, else bleeding gums. I rest my case. Do you, padre, recognise to whom I refer? If so, we have solved the identity of the graffiti artist in – let me see – under four minutes.'

'Good heavens. I know to whom you refer. I'm positive. I recall the boy's incessant wilful smoking and loitering about the graves on Tuesday last with some other youths. Tommy Weekes. His gums are sensitive and bleed so that on occasions his front teeth appear bloodied and revolting. I must away to tell his mother of her son's disgraceful behaviour.'

'Stay your hand for the present, padre. He is talented, I'll say that much for him.'

'Talented! Really, sir, sacrilegious is how I should describe his scribblings. Oh, I realise the carvings and defacings do have a certain flair for the absurd. The giant rat drawn on Mrs Lacey's front door in her own image comes to mind. But he must be punished. A breech birth as a new-born, he was delivered by forceps and this has left him a little dull-witted. His behaviour is eccentric at times. Now I must depart and prepare to deliver the news to Mrs Weekes – that her son must go round with a cloth and pail and remove these images of rats from people's property. The carvings of rodents must for the time remain.'

'One moment, vicar,' said Holmes in a con-cerned way. 'I should like as reward to be the first to interview the boy and his mother. I would be interested, during a private interview, to witness his reaction to being found out. I promise all will remain confidential and I shall report my find-ings to you later this evening.'

'That sounds fair. He lives with his mother at Thornycroft Cottage, a little way up the lane from my church. May I heartily congratulate you on solving this community matter with such élan and obvious professionalism. Your names, sirs, so that I might recall this moment for posterity.'

'Doctor Watson,' said I.

'Mr Sherlock Holmes at your service.'

'Good grief – not *the* Sherlock Holmes?'

'Just so.'

'Gentlemen, come to my rectory across the way at once. I must force a sherry on you both. I declare I am an out-and-out devotee of the *Strand* magazine and follow your articles avidly, – oh, and this evening you must join me for supper, I insist on it.'

9

Tommy Weekes's Undoing

After a short stroll up the lane, banked on either side by tall hedgerow trees, we came across the lighted window of a cottage of thatched roof and cob, set some distance from the road. The vicar had loaned us his bull's-eye lantern, for by now it was completely dark and visibility, due to the lack of street lamps in these out of the way country places, very sporadic, causing me to narrowly avoid tripping into a chicken coop as we approached the front door through the garden.

'Do come in, sirs. Would you like tea? There's plenty in the pot.'

'Thank you madam. A hot drink is most welcome on a bitter, rainy night such as this. We are new to the Broads and enjoying a bird-watching holiday. We stay at the Duck and Drake further down.'

'I will have a biscuit, thank you,' said I, warming to the lady at once. She made us feel splendidly at home and seldom have I encountered such openness and genuine hospitality.

The labourer's cottage belonging to Mrs Weekes, a washerwoman by trade, who supplemented her modest income by the sewing and mending of lace and fabrics, consisted of a front parlour that, although cramped and smoky from the coal range, was kept trim and tidy and there was a homely, welcoming atmosphere to the place. Tommy, unaware that he was about to be unmasked and suffer reprimand for his art's sake, chomped on a thick wedge of crusty loaf smothered in dripping.

'Well sirs, what can I do for thee?' asked the chubby matron, beaming with goodwill, her face lit up by the oil lamp above. 'Help your'sels to more tea.'

'We have just come from the rectory,' said Holmes, taking out his pipe and tobacco pouch and placing them upon the chequered table cloth, 'where, before taking sherry, we were given a tour of the vestry by your most courteous and engaging clergyman, the Rev. Marsden-Lee. He was anxious to show us a new portrait he had recently acquired – somewhat simplistic and yet altogether a most well orchestrated caricature. The face with its twitching whiskers stood out most particularly.'

The boy, who was by now supping tea from his mug, went very bright red in the face and managed to spill scalding hot liquid down the front of his smock.

'Look at you, Tommy, you silly nitwit. What's come over you? Drink they'se tea properly like a young gentleman, like I'se always taught you as a good ma.'

'I b'aint a nitwit,' he fumed. 'I'se cans't knock up a coffin, can't I, shave the planks, French polish the elm to a grand finish?'

'Course you can dear, now don't get riled so. I know'st Simkins our local builder and undertaker is very pleased with your standard of work and he makes all the coffins for the villages hereabouts. He is of the opinion you are a skilful, worthy craftsman, but, like I says, don't slop tea everywhere.'

'A craftsman in wood should be able to use a pen-knife else a sharp chisel most effectively. Perhaps that old windmill at Potters Ditch could do with a plank or two pegged into place,' remarked Holmes.

This time the lad visibly tensed. Once more his cheeks flushed, a quivering, nervous tic evident beneath his left eye. He scowled at my colleague, no doubt wishing he would disappear in a cloud of smoke up the chimney. He held his tea mug in a vice-like grip, so hard I thought his wraparound fingers would crack the enamel.

'I shall be brief and entirely to the point, Tommy. I think you have considerable artistic talent and will go far. But the church vestry is hardly the best backdrop for your "free-fall" masterpieces. Neither should you go round defacing headstones, else daubing paint on doors. You have left a trail of etched graffiti in your wake, my dear fellow. Youthful angst, a need to express oneself by defacing property, is hardly a new phenomenon. You are not the first young man to rebel!'

Tommy Weekes's jaw dropped. A withering sigh escaped his parted lips revealing diseased gums with a potential to bleed. He sat at table entirely undone, his shameful secret exposed.

'Fear not, the most you shall receive from this interview as punishment is washing down and re-whitewashing the vestry wall. Neither Doctor Watson nor myself have any inclination to cause either yourself or your dear mother the slightest embarrassment or harm. That said, I shall rest my case only when I have got to the bottom of why, on every occasion you choose to strike, the image is the same every time – a rat! An extremely large and ferocious rat! Apart from the matter of whitewashing the vestry wall at ten tomorrow morning, which you will perform as just penance to appease the wrath of the vicar, why I ask does the same restive image dominate your graffiti art? I put it to you, young man, something has recently upset you, some recent event has infected your creativity. I believe you know who, or what, was responsible for killing the first victim, George Flemps, up by the barn.'

'A rat!' he cried, bursting into sobs. 'I see'd a giant rat sir, honest I done. I see'd it swummin along the Broads wi' my own eyes. I bared witness to it. I did see a giant rat wi' the head of George Flemps in its jaws, I did so.'

10

Foxbury Hall

By the time we had trudged up the lane to enquire at the hall over Mr Sands's health, it was pitch black and raining heavily. Fending off the worst of the inclement weather with umbrellas borrowed from the vicar's stock of 'lost and found', brollies forgetfully mislaid on pews of a Sunday by parishioners over the years, we wondered whether the ex-M.P. might have come down here on the train from London to take up residence for the winter season, forgetting to inform the porters at Albany of his whereabouts, perhaps with the use of a basket chair, a hired invalid carriage, causing him to leave behind his usual wheeled chair at the apartment. Holmes was pretty certain this was the case, and anyhow, the Norfolk murders were of more concern and we had a full day ahead of us attending the autopsy and making more enquiries as to the violent deaths locally. The exact whereabouts of Ethby Sands was really of secondary consideration.

We came to a set of gateposts surmounted by a pair of winged gryphons and thus continued up the path until the venerable old clay-brick Norfolk mansion came into view. Foxbury Hall was, I was sure, in the sunlight of an autumn morning, an elegant home full of character and charm. Earlier I had judged the architecture to be of the Elizabethan period and the gables, diamond-pane windows and tall herringbone brick chimney stacks gave the house an air of imposing grandeur.

Once inside the porch I tugged the bell-pull and, aware of the dripping, gurgling sound of rainwater pouring off the guttering, we waited expectantly beneath the hornbeam lantern for the front door to be opened.

Soon after, a genial fellow in a frock coat, striped trousers and black tie greeted us. 'My name is Garson, sirs. How can I help? The weather at this time of year is most uncongenial and bothersome. I used to always prepare my master's hot toddy at this hour and make sure he was comfortably seated by the fire with a shawl wrapped round his shoulders.'

'Is Mr Sands at home by any chance?' asked my colleague. 'I perceive you are his valet. We were just passing and wished to convey our good wishes. He is in, presumably?'

'I regret to say, gentlemen, condolences are in order, for my master passed on at six of the clock this morning. The wasting illness from which he had suffered interminably for the last year finally claimed his life. He just had no energy left to fight it, sir. I trust you will respect the fact that the body of my master yet still resides in the house and we are all of us in a state of deep mourning. Goodnight, gentlemen, and Lord bless you for enquiring after Mr Sands at this sad time.'

'That just won't do,' my colleague remarked, showing grim fortitude as we walked back down by the shrubbery, hastening to the rectory to keep our appointment. 'A chronic invalid should not be subjected to a lengthy journey from the heart of Piccadilly to north Norfolk during autumn when the air is damp and chilly, the region steeped in marsh mist and prone to continuous drizzle. Switzerland or the Italian Alps are understandable, but East Anglia – really my dear fellow, as a doctor would you subject your patient to such unhealthy climes?'

'Absolutely not,' said I, in full agreement. 'In summer the Broads offer sailing and boating to one's heart's content, genial hours spent at the tiller exploring the channels, but at this time of year bronchial infections, stiffening of the joints –

a patient's chest in particular should be most susceptible to pneumonia. If they are already weakened and not able to eat properly, such as Ethby Sands would be, no – the vaporous, tangy air of the wetlands for a long-term sufferer such as he, I should class as positively injurious to health.'

11

The Vicar Intervenes

Having kept our appointment at the rectory, we were enjoying our evening meal. The Rev. Marsden-Lee had earlier invited us to share a repast of roast haunch of venison at the supper table in the oak-panelled dining room, prepared by his housekeeper. The candles, I confess, cast a somewhat eerie illumination on the portraits in oils of previous incumbents that were hung about the room.

'Dead!' The clergyman shrieked with laughter. 'My dear Holmes, if only you had asked, I could have told you that much and saved you both a wasted journey. The matter of Tommy Weekes was of course uppermost in our conversation when we last spoke over sherry. I myself visited Foxbury Hall this afternoon after learning of our old Norwich M.P.'s passing. Most sad, but not entirely unexpected due to his chronic state of health. But, you know, it all went rather queer.'

'What went rather queer?' said I, sampling a

glass of excellent French wine.

'We heard a rumour, a death up at the big house, Mr Sands's passing of course. Well, Mrs Lunn, our ministering angel, who does the flowers in my church, a woman of advanced years who whenever there is a death in the village takes it on herself, to prepare the deceased, washing, doing "the necessary", sheeting the corpse, making everything presentable, by no means an interfering old busybody, came to see me in floods of tears. A man up at the manor house had apparently told her to get off the property. He called her a witch!'

Holmes glanced up from his plate, his pale, sallow, aquiline features all aquiver from the wavering light of the candelabrum on our table which cast shadows about the room, making those dratted oil paintings of stern old country parsons seem alive and overly judgemental.

'Yes, I think we catch your drift, padre,' said he. 'The old lady was naturally upset by this fellow's uncouth attitude'.

'I asked her if it was not Mr Garson the valet to whom she referred. "Oh no sir," she insisted, "for he is a gentleman's gentleman, a man of impeccable manners who should never dream of addressing a lady like that. This was a young man wearing red loafers claiming to be the son."

'"But, my dear lady," I replied, "Mr Sands was a confirmed bachelor. He never married in his life and was, before his illness, fond of his clubs and fine dining. He was a fellow who as far as I know had no understanding whatsoever of the ways of a woman's heart. Garson was his only constant companion over the years, in good times and bad.

A son? Why, that's absurd! I shall ask cook to make you a very hot gin and water while I meanwhile go and give this young bounder a good talking to!"'

'Bravo! Most commendable.'

'I was appalled by the insensitive treatment of this woman who, after all, only wanted to help lay out Mr Sands with all the dignity and care she could muster, so I went up to the hall, cutting through the walled kitchen garden, and saw the back door to the house had been left open. Well, I am acquainted with Lord Astor, who rents Foxbury Hall out in the winter, and know the layout of the rooms fairly well from previous visits, so I let myself in and – what a shock – there was a group of Chinamen, I ask you, bickering with one another, consulting a map that had been laid out flat on the kitchen table, a map depicting the naked human form, indecent and covered in heretical symbols and underlinings, the diagram countenanced by numerals and Chinese letters of the alphabet. The abhorrent scent of powerful joss alerted me to Oriental mischief, wholly un-Christian ethics.'

'Practitioners of alternative medicine,' corrected my companion good-naturedly. 'They were merely discussing acupuncture, studying a chart, my dear Marsden-Lee. I have spent time in Tibet and China and can assure you there was nothing untoward regarding their activities. Do carry on. Your observations are first rate.'

'Be that as it may, Mr Holmes, I demanded to see Mr Sands's body there and then, to view the corpse.'

'Ha ha, by Jove that's good and pushy.'

'To pray for the soul of the departed, to offer up a prayer for the dead in the Anglican faith. Well, my arrival was greeted with polite disapproval. I was bustled away by their leader, a tall, gangly Chinaman, austere to the extreme with a cruel mouth and menacing airs who went by the name of Wu. Doctor Wu Xing. He was evidently held in high esteem for the other Orientals would respectfully bow when referring to this chart of blasphemy.

'I was evicted! Evicted from the hall as a trespasser. Me! The vicar of the parish and on friendly terms with Lord Astor. Well, I have not been back since.'

'Did you perchance observe anything else of interest?' asked Holmes.

'Now you come to mention it, I was passing round by the shrubbery and happened to peer into the billiard room. The windows look out onto the flower beds, and the lawn and tennis courts. Well, I chanced upon the strangest thing, for there on top of the green baize billiard table was a most peculiar receptacle. Not exactly a proper elm coffin, more of a wicker compostable shell, a lightweight coffin of basketwork favoured these days by faddish vegetarians and slavish pre-Raphaelite followers of William Morris who prefer to be buried beneath a flower bed in the garden.'

'And of the young man calling himself the son?'

'I saw nothing of him, Mr Holmes. He might well have been a complete stranger, an impostor for all we know.'

56

12

A Change of Plan

Inspector Wells called for us bright and early. We were ensconced in the snug of the Duck and Drake, eating our breakfast of ham and eggs, washed down by halves of warm beer, in front of a roaring log fire in the settle. One only had to glance out of the latticed window to confirm it was a misty, damp morning – grey and overcast.

'An autopsy is to be performed over at Walpole St Thomas at nine of the clock, gentlemen. Doctor Clayborne is anxious we should start on time. I have the horse and trap waiting.'

'Heaven forbid that we should delay proceedings, Inspector, but I fear we must return to London. There is at Albany in Piccadilly a mysterious disappearance which for now must take precedence over the Norfolk murders. After a brief walk to stretch the legs we will be departing for the station halt to catch the next London-bound train. My pocket *Bradshaw* indicates we shall be required to change at Cambridge.'

'Well, I must say, isn't that highly irregular, Mr Holmes? What can possibly take precedence over two horribly orchestrated murders?'

'Finding the perpetrator, Inspector. What else have you to tell me?'

'Well, sir, we found something interesting when

we were dredging the channel at Potters Ditch – a muddied, stout ash stick, more of a cudgel – handle of carved antler.'

'Then I suggest you check locally who might own it! Landlord, a fill of your most excellent tobacco from the jar. Please prepare our bill, for we shall be leaving presently.'

I can report, upon our return journey to Norwich, our two-coach train propelled along the branch by a light engine, both of us were avidly reading the first editions of the daily papers, the pages of which were spread over the cloth-covered seats, and little was said.

My dear friend, his charred old briar-root pipe clenched between his teeth, was smoking contentedly, filling our compartment with the reek of coarse country inn tobacco. I tamped down strands of my own preferred Arcadia mixture into the bowl of my pipe and struck a match, glad to be leaving behind the dreary scene of the Broads and returning home to Baker Street.

We caught an express at Cambridge and as we rattled along, Holmes, as he was wont to do, while scowling at the obituary notices, proceeded to underline a section of print with his propelling pencil and passed me the folded newspaper. I was thus able to become further acquainted with the life and times of Ethby Sands, once an M.P. for Norwich, who owned a fabulous collection of rare, stuffed birds of paradise and had also, it seemed, notably composed a best-selling hymn tune. There was the proper mention of his final days, the enduring struggle he put up against the virulent form of wasting disease, and the correspondent ended with 'Died peacefully in the early hours with his beloved valet Mr Henry Garson by his bedside at the country seat of Lord Astor in the county of Norfolk.'

'A complete and utter fabrication, my dear Watson, cleverly placed in this morning's edition of the *Telegraph*. No doubt all the broadsheets bear testimony to his life ... and death. His admirers shall genuinely mourn his passing. His detractors wholly welcome it.'

'Detractors – who are they?' I asked.

'At present I am not at liberty to say. Once we have returned to the capital, might I bother you to accompany me to the Royal Geographical Society in Exhibition Road?'

'Certainly,' said I, continuing to stare out of the compartment window.

13

The Royal Geographical Society

The fog lay thick and dun-coloured, blanketing the metropolis, making visibility poor and our journey across London from the station slow as to be almost futile. East of the Albert Hall it took us over an hour to reach the Royal Geographical Society. We were stuck in a jam, with carriage, omnibus and dray traffic virtually at a standstill.

'Why on earth are we visiting the R.G.S.?' said I, while our cab rattled up Exhibition Road and our goal was at last in sight, the familiar red-brick Queen Ann façade coming up on our right. 'I have seen no lectures advertised. Drat it old man, I should have preferred to spend my time as an idler perusing my latest edition of the *British Medical Journal* before the homely hearth. Have we not had enough action for one week? Those infernal Broads of north Norfolk – two unsolved murders – no, I am annoyed my familiar bachelor routine should be disrupted like this.'

'Fear not old man. I have in my mind a rather pressing matter concerning old maps and log-books that needs attending to.'

'Old maps, logbooks? I don't follow.'

'I am merely curious to delve more fully into the matter of the island of Sumatra.'

'Not those blasted stuffed birds of paradise again! Really Holmes, you are the limit!'

Cedric Bitten, the long-serving secretary and senior librarian, an epitome of jolly eccentricity, brimming with fascinating information, led us into the map room. He proved most courteous and civil and knew both Holmes and myself by sight, for we had attended various exhibitions and lectures over the years, including those of David Livingstone and Fridtjof Nansen, the Norwegian Arctic explorer.

Stooping over, the frock-coated gentleman, half blind from years of study as an Oxbridge don, wore the thickest-lensed spectacles I ever saw. He beckoned us to a table and awaited Holmes's request with great patience and dignity.

'My dear Bitten, I am indebted to your unsurpassed knowledge of travel books and maps. This sounds trite to the extreme and I must profusely apologise in advance for such a nonsensical waste of your valuable scholarship – but have you in your long experience as R.G.S. librarian ever come across the image mark of a rat?'

'Gabriel Doppelmayer's celestial chart of 1742 shows a curious rat and we do possess an early sixteenth-century Portuguese map which depicts a caricature, a replication of a giant rodent positioned above one of the remote Indonesian islands, or Muluccas, as is their proper title.'

'Sumatra,' said I, hardly believing my ears. 'Sixteenth century you say?'

'Just so, Doctor Watson. Be good enough to wait here. I shall ask young Credon, our junior clerk, to fetch the appropriate folder from the rack. Would either of you perchance like a cup of coffee? It is devilishly foggy and your journey over here from the station terminus must have been fraught with delays at every turn.'

'Most kind,' replied Holmes. He warmed his hands in front of the vast ornamental mantelpiece, a crackling fire in the grate. Paintings in oil of famous explorers and past presidents of the Society graced the oak-panelled room.

Our genial librarian shuffled off to fetch coffee and biscuits.

'You know, my dear Watson, Bitten is really a most amazing fellow. His brain is quite the finest storage facility for facts concerning geography and antiquated travel books, logs and documents I have yet to come across. I am not saying he is on a par with brother Mycroft, who possesses the most retentive brain attic in all England, able to simultaneously analyse and store myriad facts and figures and details of minutiae – but Bitten is close, damn close. Ah, thank you, Credon. Here Watson, our map has arrived, neatly bound in tooled green Morocco, I perceive.'

Holmes raised his magnifying lens and together we leant over and carefully studied this very old and rare coloured map of the tropics.

'We have it Watson, we have it!' my colleague said at length, excitedly seizing my arm. He was jubilant, for there, drawn across one of the beautifully colour-tinted islands was clearly a ferocious looking rodent of massive proportions – a terrified native Sumatran clamped between its bloody jaws, filthy, sharp incisors buried into the poor fellow's neck. He was about to be devoured while other natives looked on, surrounding the giant rat and brandishing primitive spears and a net.

Bitten returned with our refreshments. 'Might I just mention in passing, gentlemen, the word "giant" is but a loose generalisation. The proper translation is "great and munificent". Thus you can infer from this illustration that the native population not only hunted this rodent but also revered it.'

Bitten indicated a plate of biscuits and passed us each a cup of coffee from the tray. Thereafter, craning his neck and refocusing those pebbly lenses of his on the map he commented with obvious disdain, 'Peculiar creature – represented as a carnivore, a man-eater. Tut tut, really, that is taking liberties!'

'The ears are certainly longer and hairier than

the common black rat that so infests our London sewers,' I remarked, sipping my coffee.

'Yellow, gingery fur, mottled to form patches of white, Watson!' said my colleague enthusiastically.

'Now, now gentlemen,' warned Bitten, 'you must proceed delicately. You, Mr Holmes, are speaking as though "Ratty" here were real, that the species actually exists. This just won't do. The trained cartographer would regard this caricature with justified scepticism.' He paused to take a sip of coffee. 'Map artists in the sixteenth century were notoriously inaccurate and took untold liberties. The rat is probably nothing like depicted here.'

'In this instance I'm not sure the illustrator did not get it exactly right,' said Holmes, a worried expression surfacing on his hawk-like features. 'Now, on to the printed word, Mr Bitten.'

'Mr Holmes, I have already instructed young Credon to extract from the library shelves a number of suitable volumes – naval documents recording early voyages to the spice islands – copies of course, the originals being way too fragile to handle.'

Credon duly provided us with copies of the aforementioned documentation. One extract from a logbook belonging to a Captain Dreyfuss Malmby RN., particularly caught our interest. Written in brown, watery ink with a quill pen, each page meticulously recorded an expedition by a group of officers and ratings who first came ashore to the island of Sumatra in a row-boat armed with pistols and muskets, evidently fearing the worst. But those fears proved ungrounded.

Our vessel Bulldog *safely anchored in the bay. Upon landing on the island named Sumatra I am thus pleased and gratified to report no hostility did we encounter, rather the natives appeared both friendly and industrious, eager to trade for a variety of fish, fruit and much-prized spices, in exchange for tobacco and iron cooking utensils. A peculiarity upon which we all remarked was the fact that on our trip not one old or ailing person did we encounter. Even in the village of palm huts it appeared age and infirmity had been banished for no old people were to be seen, neither sleeping, cooking nor going about their business. Village elders, so much a part of Indonesian culture, the mainstay of a community, were entirely absent. I thus congratulated the chief amongst this tribe of young men and women through a translator, and heartily commended the health and wellbeing thereof. Grinning, he pointed to a cooking pot and flayed animal skins drying out, hung from poles. These rough, hairy hides were evidently precious to them.*

Our initial fears that the old and infirm were, at a certain advanced age, led away to a jungle clearing and left to be devoured by predatory beasts as in certain other tropical cultures were mercifully proved unfounded for I was assured that by consuming the flesh of a giant tree-rat who inhabited this island exclusively, youth and vitality were maintained and that the bones of that same animal when ground down to a fine powder could enable a man or woman to live to be three hundred years of age, and that most of the islanders had never known a day's illness in their lives, the average age being two hundred and fifty years.

The meat, I doth report to my king, be tough and inedible, though sampling a sip of the special potion they talked of, the effects upon the bowels were most agreeable and filled us with a sense of wellbeing and wonder at our situation.

Ratings and officers alike, we rowed back to our sailing barque in good spirits with eight native palm baskets brimful of spices.

Ship's Doctor's Report: H.M.S. *Bulldog*

After a most thorough examination of the returning crew, ratings and gentlemen officers alike, I confess dear brethren I am at a complete loss to explain exactly how the older ratings (indeed our captain himself is nine and fifty years of age) seemed verily sunnier and full of much youthful exuberance. Their physical ailments and grumpy demeanour so evident before their departure in the row-boat are replaced by muscular suppleness, youthful faces and they are so jolly and overbearing as to cause me great displeasure and to become irritable and off-hand with them.

The ratings and officers I examined showed much signs of increased vitality and strength since visiting the island called Sumatra. Am I, a man of science and medicine, to wholly support such unnatural change in a man, else as I suspect some diabolical, un-Christian sorcery may be at work?

'What are we to make of this, Holmes?' said I, placing my coffee cup back on the tray in a state of continuing puzzlement.

'The evidence mounts up, my dear fellow,' said Holmes with a frown. 'It is obvious to me Ethby

Sands has given himself over to some dastardly medical experiment. His absence from Albany this last fortnight, the time spent in Norfolk holed up at Foxbury Hall bodes ill.'

'You infer this group of Chinese led by Doctor Wu Xing, the alternative medicine crowd, may have succeeded in producing a viable serum that duplicates in modern terms the effects of the native potion of powdered bone?'

'I do, Watson, I do old man. Come, we must make haste in a cab to the telegraph office. There is a person who above all others can enlighten us further concerning this peculiar case.'

14

Alfred Russell Wallace

Less than a week later, I recall as if yesterday, a slender, tall gentleman with a nut-brown complexion, sporting a long bushy beard and round wire-rimmed spectacles entered our rooms at Baker Street. He had been guided up the stairs by Mrs Hudson, who I could see was in complete awe of our visitor, and with good reason, for here in our modest bachelor apartment we now played host to the explorer and naturalist, the author of *The Malay Archipelago*, Alfred Russell Wallace; he who had been a close friend of Darwin and at great cost to his own health and personal finances had single-handedly explored some of the remotest islands on earth.

It was a rare privilege indeed to receive his Panama hat and brolly and, once he was comfortably seated before a blazing fire in the grate, offer him a cigar from the coal scuttle, while Holmes poured us each a glass of whisky. My colleague had arranged this interview with the great man at very short notice, Wallace being down in London for the opening night of a new light opera at the Wimborne, Drury Lane, written of course by the lyricist Philip Troy and composer Christopher Chymes.

We had ourselves been invited and were fortunate enough that same evening to attend, sharing a box with Wallace, his wife Annie and their daughter Violet and sons Herbert and William, who had come up from Cornwall specially and were staying for a day or two at the Langham. Once we were all settled, Holmes fastidiously refilled his pipe and, languidly stretching his long legs across the bearskin hearthrug, posed his first question of the evening.

'I recall noting in your autobiography, Wallace, that you went down with a serious fever some time in 1858. You nearly lost your life due to malnutrition and the onset of a severe strain of malaria. You lay on your cot drifting in and out of consciousness for many days and nights in that time, but you received an unusual visitor, a shaman from the Indonesian island of Sumatra.'

'To an explorer in the tropics, as I then was Mr Holmes, the unseen dangers of semi-starvation and disease are always present. I was at the time, you will recall, lying on a cot-bed in a palm-thatched house, dangerously ill, hallucinating, my feeble constitution unable to stave off a virulent bout of yellow fever. I must emphasise, gentlemen, that had it not been for the intervention of this native, an accomplished shaman, I believe I should have died and been lost to hoards of black ants, giant centipedes and carnivorous termites who abound in that region of the interior, and would certainly never have made it back to England alive.'

'A shaman, you say,' said I, taking notes in my little pocketbook.

'Indeed, Doctor Watson, I had long known the Albverro of Seram, for instance, were renowned and powerful magicians and spirit guides. But it was a bird trader of all people with whom I had been doing business, who happened to be visiting Sumatra and, using all his influence, persuaded this powerful shaman (for a substantial consignment of rare bird feathers) to travel across the islands on a trading *prahu* and visit me. So there was I, suffering dysentery and a high fever, sweltering in that damn palm hut, when this kindly native shows up. I barely registered his presence at first. I recall a happy, dusky fellow patting me on the shoulder, allowing some sweat from my brow to trickle into a tiny clay pot he kept strung around his neck. My native visitor lost no time in assessing my condition and it was lucky he acted so promptly. From beneath his shawl he drew out a bundle of brittle old bones wrapped in the stiffened, mummified hide of some long dead animal. A horribly squashed head, large furry ears, a compressed snarling snout, the vilest looking, longest and sharpest incisors I ever saw. The acute smell of the matted fur, the leathery skin, repulsed me.

'"Take it away," I exclaimed, more dead than alive. "Take the damn thing away and burn it." The native found my feverish ranting highly amusing and chuckled merrily, once more patting me on the shoulder and emitting a *chuk-chuk-chuk, chuk-chuk-chuk* from between pursed lips, quickly followed by a peculiar keening noise such as a rodent makes, which seemed to soothe away my fevered thoughts and calm my inner being wonderfully. I slept soundly and deeply for the first time in weeks, awaking now and then to find my new friend, my surrogate mother if you will, squatted on his haunches, busily occupied with pestle and mortar, grinding bony fragments from that awful emasculated creature into a fine powder which he then placed in a jar and mixed with a quantity of blood drawn by hideous slug-like leeches cleaving to my inner thigh, to form a mash to which he added water.

'The shaman would occasionally allow me a sip of this potion, else feed me slices of a delicious fruit entirely unknown to me.'

'This animal – would you classify it as a rat?'

'Why yes, Mr Holmes, a giant tree-rat native only to Sumatra, a species rare and long extinct, an exotic specimen. I grant you that if I had been in my right senses and able to think straight, and record jottings in my journal of travels properly, or even write a paper on it, I might have regarded the specimen as a valuable link in the evolutionary chain. At the time my dear friend, Charles

Darwin, was as you know busy embarking upon his great work *On the Origin of Species,* and perhaps if I had been more my old self I would have drawn his attention to the giant Indonesian tree-rat earlier. As it was, I loathed the sight of the filthy-smelling vermin. However, gentlemen, when it came time for Samu the shaman to leave, and I was fully recovered, he left the skin and bones for me and I had not the heart to throw them out or destroy them. So Samu, that dear, beloved companion of mine for so long, left me the tree-rat remains as a present – a gift to recall our association – and they got placed in a bamboo crate and were all but forgotten, until my eventual return to these shores. It was only when I began to classify and label my finds back in London, and by this time I was a happily married man, that the old bones, wrapped in animal hide, once more came to prominence. I recall my darling wife found the items stuffed behind one of my portmanteaux. She picked up the rolled-up carcass of matted hair and calcified bone, commenting about the awful snout and teeth the creature possessed. She said, "I don't care if it's a rare Sumatran tree rat, Alfred, for goodness sake get rid of it. The old skin and bone pongs to high heaven and should be heaped on the bonfire, I don't want it in the house. I dread to think what dormant mites and ticks it is host to."

'Of course I did not even then want to destroy the specimen so we contacted Charles Darwin and his wife and they agreed to take it off my hands.'

'Now we come to the crux of the matter,

Wallace. We know much about your giant tree-rat of Sumatra but next to nothing about the potion. Another whisky?'

'I will have another, thank you Holmes. All right, the potion – well, I can honestly say hand on heart it worked. If there is such a thing as the elixir of eternal youth, this gets damnably close. Not only did it contain healing properties, but when I next looked in the glass after being confined to my cot with yellow fever, for God knows how long and close to death, I had lost middle age and become young again. I felt cleansed, entirely rejuvenated in both body and mind. Samu the shaman insisted he had lived three hundred years, and amongst his tribe on Sumatra he was but a young man, a mere whippersnapper.'

'But, scientifically, surely that's unfeasible – an anti-ageing potion belongs to Greek myth,' said I, stubbing out the remains of my cigar in the ashtray.

'Make of it what you will, gentlemen,' said he at length, sipping from his glass. 'But I tell you truthfully, it proved effective.'

'One more thing Wallace.'

'By all means.'

'If it were possible, say, to replicate this potion you talk of, to produce a modern serum from the remains of this long-extinct tree-rat, who would you plump for, who should possess the requisite skills and knowledge to carry it through?'

'The Chinese come to mind. As a race they are so far advanced in alternative medicine. One only has to visit a Chinese herbalist in Limehouse to see the similarities.'

15

Opening Night

The theatre lights dimmed. We took our places in the box. Alfred Wallace, his wife and family filed in and took their seats. We were all of us expectantly passing round a bag of mint humbugs, making sure our opera glasses were close at hand. At last the performance got under way. A rousing overture, both instantly melodic and catchy, set our feet tapping and hands clapping to the infectious rhythm of the orchestra in the pit, being conducted by Sir Penfold Wilkes in white tie and tails. A stirring baton-led march led to the curtains parting on an idyllic tropical island. A gorgeous young lady walked hand in hand beneath the coconut palms with her handsome beau and a love duet ensued.

'By Jove,' said I to Alfred Wallace in the next seat. 'That's the second catchy tune and we're barely into the first act.'

'Agreed,' said he, nodding his head, his spectacles flashing in the subdued wall lighting. 'I think they have a hit on their hands, Doctor Watson.'

Entranced, we sat in the box, occasionally moved to tears, as stirring rumbustious marches alternated with tuneful ballads and Bella eventually promised eternal fidelity and marriage to young

Archie, a poor rating whose ship would be leaving for England the next day, leaving the pretty young maiden alone to pine for her love. She, the daughter of a cantankerous, possessive widower, a hypochondriac moaner, a gruff old Welsh missionary by the name of Davies, played to perfection by our dear friend Charles Lemon.

The first act went riotously well and we sat enthralled. The second act, however, seemed to fall short. I should mention we were by then introduced to a chorus of cuddly dancing giant rats who sang of the delights of an idyllic tropical island.

'Sumatra, Sumatra, Sumatran jolly rats are we. Paradise is ours, the sun, the palms and the sea.'

Tosh, of course, but the younger members of the audience lapped it up, screaming and wildly applauding every time the blasted rodents made an appearance. I perceived the more mature members of the audience found the cuddly toy rats annoying after a while and I heard much coughing and blowing of noses.

The light opera, a musical entertainment in the style of Gilbert and Sullivan, else Franz Lehar, was well directed and had much to commend it. This said, those wretched singing and dancing giant rats spoiled it for me. I should rather have seen more of the beautiful, leggy chorus girls dressed in grass skirts.

By the last act, however, the musical had gloriously improved and even though the giant rats appeared in the finale, the final, uplifting duet where young Archie, now a naval lieutenant, returns to Sumatra and rescues Bella from the cooking pot, was superb. He sang poignantly the words: '*Sumatra, Sumatra, I met the love of my life here, I have eyes only for you dearest dear, dearest Bella, my Bella, my sweetest Bella dear.*'

This brought the house down. We all stood up and applauded till our hands hurt. Everyone in the theatre was on their feet for a last rousing, foot-stomping rendition of the catchy overture.

After the last bow, the applause gently dying away while the house gas jets came up, we made our way downstairs to congratulate the composer Christopher Chymes and lyricist Philip Troy and break a bottle of champagne with the impresario of the Wimborne, Langton Lovell and his business partner Charles Lemon, who had played the old missionary, Davies, with such zeal and flair. Unfortunately, a terrible tragedy then occurred, which marred proceedings somewhat.

I recall as if yesterday, Holmes and myself, arm in arm, some way behind Alfred Russell Wallace and his family being led along a backstage corridor full of props and actors congratulating one another, when from a room at the end a very shocked and pale looking Christopher Chymes emerged, being supported by Langton Lovell.

'Philip is dead,' the composer gasped, clutching at his friend's sleeve, tears forming in the corners of his eyes. 'Poor Troy's dead.'

'A heart failure,' said I, rushing forward. 'Christopher, I am a doctor, we may be able to yet resuscitate him. Lead the way old man.'

'No point. He's been murdered,' he cried. 'Oh dear God, his throat's clawed through, there's so much blood, up the walls, the lino. The room's been ransacked!'

'Steady Christopher,' said Langton, leading Chymes over to a props trunk, insisting he should sit down and gather composure. 'Brandy, someone – a dashed large measure. Hurry!'

While Wallace and his family were ushered away I was annoyed when a tall Chinaman in flowing silk robes and wearing a pill-box hat barged right past us without a by-your-leave, dashing into the recently vacated murder room.

'Where is he? Where is my patient?' he said, more to himself than us, his noble Oriental features clouding over into a protracted scowl. His thin, cruel mouth pursed slightly. He shook his head and was about to depart through the crowd of horrified onlookers gathering in the corridor when, brandishing his sword stick, Holmes promptly blocked his path.

'Doctor Wu Xing, I presume?' said my companion, peering into the Chinaman's face intently. 'You will do me the honour of accompanying myself and Doctor Watson back to Baker Street. We have much to discuss. If you want to avoid the police and remain at liberty in the foreseeable future I strongly advise you to comply. A four-wheeler shall convey us swiftly to Marylebone. Theatre land must, for now alas, be forsaken, perhaps prudent, for the Wimborne shall soon become awash with the denizens of Fleet Street after a story, and Scotland Yard to examine the murder scene. Do I make myself plain?'

'Undoubtedly. Come gentlemen, I am no Malay or Chinese coolie from East India Docks, neither do I frequent the opium dens of Limehouse. We are civilised human beings. Lead the way, Mr Sherlock Holmes. I have long been acquainted with your redoubtable reputation as the capital's greatest and only serving consulting detective. Doctor Watson, I feel privileged to meet you, albeit in questionable circumstances.'

'Compliments and flattery aside, you are in very deep, Doctor Wu. Your patient is I believe reliably responsible for two brutal murders in Norfolk and now this debacle, this bloodbath backstage at the Wimborne.'

We flagged down a cab outside the theatre. There was mayhem, crowds of morbid sight-seers, descending on the Wimborne as though for a show of carnage at the Roman Coliseum. Word had got out that Philip Troy, responsible for writing the lyrics to the latest smash musical *The Giant Rats of Sumatra,* had been murdered back stage. I was glad to be quitting the West End for it seemed to me under the gas lamps that people looked as ghoulish and hungry as marauding vampires, eager to be somehow part of this event, to be involved and able to say, 'Look at me – I was there.' No, I confess I was glad to get out. No doubt Inspector Lestrade would be leading an investigation into the matter. Good luck to him. Holmes and myself had bigger fish to fry for Doctor Wu Xing represented a breakthrough. How I longed to hear what he had to relate concerning his controversial patient.

'A monster,' the Chinaman murmured, smoking an exotic, perfumed cigarette from an ivory holder carved with writhing black bears locked in combat. As our four-wheeler rattled along Drury

76

Lane towards High Holborn, we were at last able to gain speed once we extricated ourselves from the jam of omnibuses and carriages along by the Theatre Royal.

'Pardon me?' said I, peering out as the dun-coloured fog, less persistent, lifted in places so that I could see we were approaching Long Acre upon our left.

'A monster smash, Doctor Watson. Nothing shall stop the publicity machine now. Demand for tickets shall be phenomenal.'

'Indeed,' remarked Holmes, puffing on his pipe as our cab clattered through foggy London, on-wards towards Oxford Street.

16

Doctor Wu Explains

Once indoors in the familiar surroundings of our diggings in Baker Street, blinds drawn, lamps lit, cosily aglow, a good fire raging in the grate, Holmes poured us each a glass of whisky. He charged his long cherry-wood pipe with the strongest shag from the Persian slipper attached to the corner of our mantelpiece and, once he was sat cross-legged in his favourite armchair beside the hearth, gently began to probe the clever if con-ceited mind of the Chinese doctor of alternative medicine.

'You have a clinic, I believe?'

'Yes, in Mayfair – in a brick and stucco terrace off Regent Street.'

'Plagiarism – stolen ideas – that's where part of the problem of this confounded multi-faceted puzzle of murder and bodily rejuvenation lies, is it not Doctor Wu Xing?'

'You are of course correct, Mr Holmes. The original idea for the light opera that I am sure both of you enjoyed this evening at the Wimborne, came from Ethby Sands. Perhaps you noticed a japanned upright piano he keeps in the bay in his sitting room at Albany. It possesses pleasant memories for him and has a very impressive history. When he first visited my clinic he told me how, as a young man, he was a passable pianist. He could play Chopin or a ragtime tune for friends at a supper party. He was not of a professional standard and was entirely self-taught.

'One winter's afternoon he claimed to me he saw the face of his long dead mother in the gilt mirror and was instantly moved to sit on the stool and randomly play at scales. He swears, gentlemen, that in under ten minutes he composed a catchy hymn tune, that at first he was convinced he must have heard before at a concert or choral gathering, or at a church. He wrote down the music upon the back of a cigarette packet and thought no more of it until, when entertaining some fellow residents in Albany he played it to the conductor Lonsdale Chymes, who instantly said he had a smash. The rest, as they say, is music publishing history. The Americans loved it, church choirs loved it, orchestras performed the piece, and even today it remains a popular tune played in front rooms throughout the land. Boosey & Hawkes have so far sold thirty million copies of the sheet music and counting. The title 'Take Thy Tiny Hand in Mine' was likewise Ethby's, who of course wrote both words and music to his 'little ditty' as he fondly referred to the hymn.'

'So Christopher's father Lonsdale forms a link. It was the famous orchestra conductor who advised Ethby Sands, and you could say was partly responsible for the tune's success,' asked Holmes.

'Lonsdale, through his music contacts, championed the song. He was very generous in his praise of the hymn and must have helped its path considerably,' replied Doctor Wu.

'And the son Christopher, who himself resides at Albany, using his father's apartment, wanted Ethby Sands dead. He and Philip Troy presumably stole the idea for the show *The Giant Rats of Sumatra*.'

'Listen,' sighed Wu, 'that plain and simple hymn dwarfed any of the achievements of Christopher Chymes and Philip Troy. A modest reputation they had as a songwriting team, certainly. They'd played as a duo at the Ritz and small venues, showcasing their material. But neither had hit the big money and they wanted in on celebrity and fame. However, neither Chymes nor Troy had a core idea, something to get theatre producers and impresarios knocking at their door. One evening they had a bachelor's supper with Ethby Sands at his upstairs set. He was of course at the time an M.P. for Norwich and busy with affairs of constituency and Parliament. There was even talk that one day he might become a cabinet minister.

Anyhow, they all got drunk and he got up and played them a tune on the 'old Joanna' and (foolishly he admits this) somewhat tight from too much wine and champagne confided to them his gay and romping tour de force, a light opera set on a paradise island in Indonesia – the island of Sumatra – but his biggest and most brilliant flash of inspiration was the inclusion of a chorus of giant cuddly rats.'

'And this is where Alfred Russell Wallace comes in,' said I, understanding at last.

'Charles Darwin had been offered an animal hide wrapped around some old bones, purportedly belonging to a now extinct species of Sumatran tree-rat – an enormous rodent. For some reason he decided to sell the items, once the property of the naturalist and explorer Alfred Wallace, who had recently returned to England after a lengthy sojourn in the tropics. A London museum was the first choice but in the end it was Ethby Sands who purchased these extraordinary items for one hundred guineas. He kept them displayed in a glass cabinet for years – a curiosity – a conversation piece. Sometimes people would glance at the mummified skin and bone and comment on it. But when Ethby Sands came to be gravely ill, near death, and all the specialists in Harley Street had given up on him, he remembered its curious and spectacular provenance.'

'I must be frank with you Doctor Wu, I have already interviewed Alfred Wallace who was, along with his family, down from Cornwall to see the play. At the Royal Geographical Society I have seen the rat with my own eyes, drawn on a sixteenth-century Portuguese map – a caricature of a giant rat, disturbingly and horribly portrayed by the illustrator. I can only draw the following conclusion. Somehow you and your team of microscopic chemists, who are specialised practitioners of Chinese alternative medicine, have managed to duplicate the Indonesian shaman's anti-ageing formula, based on grinding down the bone of this long extinct creature to form a compound of fine powder to which you add further ingredients.

'At a time when Mr Sands had virtually given up all hope, as a last resort he decided to visit your radical clinic in Mayfair, and you and your team were able to somehow keep his wasting illness at bay and make him a young man again. But what you had not taken into account was the addictive nature of the serum and the fact that it produced terrible side-effects, the rat's genes gradually infecting and eventually taking over his physical self, making him volatile, unbelievably aggressive and a predatory killing machine. Face it Doctor Wu Xing, you and your team have created a monster, sir, a person who, when dominated by this Sumatran rat's genes, will kill mercilessly without fear or favour.'

'When I first examined my patient he was suffering from a virulent strain of wasting disease. He was fifty-three but aged beyond his years, the ravages of the illness having left him wheelchair-bound and almost without energy to eat properly or digest the food so necessary to sustain life. It was when I performed the first phase of detoxification that I of course discovered he was initially being poisoned by an outside source. Antimony was present in his blood stream, gentlemen, and when I informed him of this he balled his fists and tears ran down his cheeks.'

'"My valet Garson has betrayed me," he stuttered, "but it is Chymes and Troy who want me out of the way most. Heal me, doctor, make me whole again so I may have my revenge, my just revenge. Go to my rented house in Norfolk – Foxbury Hall – money is no object. You have the old rat's skin and bone, the provenance, the handwritten account by my dear friend Alfred Wallace detailing his miraculous recovery, the life-giving force for renewal the potion contained. Do it before it is too late. You have my complete trust. I am confident you will succeed."'

17

Journey To Down House

Thus it was proposed to take a railway journey down to Kent to visit Charles Darwin's widow. By this time, the year being 1887 when this case I am writing of first came to the attention of Mr Sherlock Holmes, the famous author and naturalist had been dead these last five years. His legacy to Wallace was immense for he, along with his neighbour John Lubbock, who owned three hundred acres of land adjacent to Down House, Darwin's family home, petitioned our Prime Minister Gladstone to provide his old friend with a civil pension, which was most agreeable, for Wallace did not have a salaried job and had lost money in stocks and shares.

Down House, with its delightful prospect, pretty garden and paved walk, proved a very homely and comfortable residence, and I was particularly moved, nay impressed, by the great man's study where he wrote up all his research into the origin of species. One could almost feel his presence there, still studiously at work at his desk.

'Welcome Mr Holmes. My dear departed husband and I were always most entertained by the fire of an evening reading aloud your various adventures, so aptly recorded for posterity by your acclaimed biographer Doctor Watson. Would you both like a pot of Earl Grey?' She rang a bell that summoned a maid who hurried away to prepare the tea things.

We settled down on a comfy sofa before the sitting room fire.

'And how may I help you? Your letter was a trifle vague.'

'Alfred Wallace mentioned the other evening he had come into the possession of a peculiar mummified animal skin wrapped around a set of old bones. A shaman from the island of Sumatra presented him with this queer trophy upon his recovery from a virulent strain of yellow fever from which he nearly died.'

'I remember, Charles and I were most relieved to learn of his surviving the illness. He suffered terribly from tropical ulcers on his legs and could barely crawl across the hut in which he sought refuge. That was in 1858 I believe, on one of the remotest Indonesian islands.'

'Do you perchance know what became of that bundle of old bones, Mrs Darwin?'

'I have more than an inkling. I well recall how repulsive the items were and, like dear Annie, Alfred's wife, I would not allow Charles to bring them into the house. You must understand, the place was already crammed with umpteen specimens, and research material took up every available space. There was just no room. The book he was then writing meant he must needs be surrounded by so much clutter. But, there you are.'

'What did your husband make of the specimen?'

'I will be completely frank, Mr Holmes. Upon close inspection he was at first of the opinion that the remains of the rodent were very ancient and unique to the evolutionary chain. And indeed the giant Sumatran tree-rat presented him with much to ponder. He remained in an intense fever of excitement for a day or two at least. However, after a visit to Down House by his friend, the Irish anthropologist and zoologist Sir Terence Maguire, an eminent member of the Royal Geographical Society to whom he presented the animal hide for appraisal, Charles changed his mind and, despite its provenance and associations with the spice islands of Indonesia, believed the rodent's skin to have been cleverly manipulated, sewn together to form this large, terrifying beast. A fake in other words, a novelty, possibly used in magic ceremonies as a hex – a harbinger of ill luck.'

'So it was dismissed.'

'Forthwith, Doctor Watson. We contacted

Alfred's agent and suggested he might dispose of it for us – sell the item for say a hundred guineas to a museum and pass the proceeds on to Wallace, who had only recently returned to England from the tropics and was in need of money.'

'Did the agent manage to make a sale?' Holmes asked.

'We were contacted shortly after and the agent informed us that the M.P. Ethby Sands had agreed to purchase the item together with the provenance and personal written account of the almost fatal illness from which Wallace made such a miraculous recovery. Ethby was well known to us because he was always helping Wallace out, funding his long absences from home by the welcome purchase of rare bird skins, birds of paradise which he would stuff and have mounted for display at Albany. I do not know what became of the old bones and animal hide after that, Mr Holmes.'

18

Lunch at the Criterion

The following morning Doctor Wu Xing visited our diggings with an urgent request. We were to meet Ethby Sands at noon for lunch at the Criterion restaurant, Mr Sands apparently anxious to allay any fears we might have that he was in fact a mutable rat or a raving madman, out of control and capable of committing murder.

This ridiculous state of affairs caused the Chinese physician and my colleague to fear that an attempt on Christopher Chymes's life may have been the real motivation for this lunchtime invitation.

The composer, although busy with press interviews and putting some last-minute touches to the score of the sensational new musical that had taken the West End by storm, helped of course by the ensuing publicity in all the morning editions concerning the grisly murder of Philip Troy, that would ensure a long and profitable run both here and on Broadway, agreed to meet Holmes, myself and Doctor Wu at the Criterion, No. 224 Piccadilly, for this impromptu luncheon, the involvement of Mr Sands kept deliberately from him.

When the composer arrived, flanked by Langton Lovell and Charles Lemon, bottles of Moet were instantly uncorked. We all settled down beneath the remarkable Byzantine-style gilded ceiling for a first-rate meal, our convivial conversation interrupted when a row broke out between Holmes and Christopher Chymes, for my colleague had decided there and then to confront the young composer over his ill usage of Ethby Sands, and plagiarism of certain of his ideas. Langton and Lemon loved a theatrical spat, and looked on with quiet amusement. My colleague gave no quarter.

'Chymes, you are the worst blackguard I ever knew, defrauding poor old Ethby Sands out of royalties and, worse still, along with your collaborator Troy, seeking to deliberately steal all his ideas for your wretched musical entertainment which, as we now know, is wildly popular and assured of making a fortune at the box office.'

'You mustn't speak ill of the dead, Holmes. Troy is no more – murdered on the very eve of his triumph. I shan't admit to anything.'

'We must gain you time, Chymes. Your very life may depend upon it. You are, I am afraid, in imminent danger of extinction. Scotland Yard must be in on this, your set at Albany put under twenty-four hour watch. I choose not to go into the many particulars. Suffice to say Ethby Sands is alive. He is due to attend this luncheon at the Criterion presently.'

'Alive! That can't be the case. I read his obituary in *The Times* only the other day, Holmes.'

'Listen, he is being kept alive and youthful by an infernal serum compounded from the ancient bones of a long extinct giant tree-rat of Sumatra, not I might add the cute and fluffy caprices we saw cavorting about the stage in your show on opening night. The serum was developed at a location in Norfolk by a clever group of microscopic chemists under the leadership of Doctor Wu Xing, himself an unorthodox practitioner of alternative Chinese medicine with a clinic in Mayfair. Doctor Wu Xing saved him from being poisoned and additionally helped save his life, but at tremendous cost. The terrible side-effects of the previously untested serum are truly fearful to behold, the risks of addiction underestimated. Although no longer middle-aged and a young man again, his mind and metabolism are irrevocably altered. Doctor Wu blames overuse of the serum. Too high a dosage has at times created a change in the man's physical self.'

'My God, you mean he's changed? Ethby's changed into a raving, psychotic madman?'

'How can I make you understand, Chymes? There can be no turning back. There is no known antidote, or cure. The animal proclivities grow ever stronger.'

Out of the corner of my eye I observed a fellow wearing a hefty tweed overcoat, muffled up against the worst of the wintry weather, the chilly November fogs, with a thick wrap-around scarf, low-brimmed hat and pigskin gloves. It had to be Ethby Sands. He entered the Criterion, pausing over by the cashier's desk. An immaculately liveried waiter instantly approached but the new diner would brook no disrobing and, with a peculiar lurching gait, came across to our table.

'Hello Chymes, Holmes, Doctor Watson. You too, Lovell, Lemon; and there of course sits Doctor Wu. Delighted you could all make it at such short notice. Damn chilly this morning,' he said good-naturedly, 'The fog lies thick along the embankment and the circus is all snarled up with carriage traffic.'

'Would you remove your gloves, Mr Sands?' asked Holmes in a determined way, instantly getting up from his chair and cautiously sliding across to our fellow diner. I knew from experience my friend had already made a brief assessment of the chap's character and had found something wanting. 'I can't abide people who will insist on lunching with their gloves on, especially in such a prestigious restaurant as the Criterion. Watson, your revolver. Clamp it against his spine, there's a good fellow.'

I leapt up and did just as Holmes requested, much to the amazement of Langton and Lemon, who sat with mouths agape, their meals temporarily abandoned, horrified at my lack of decorum and the impertinence.

'No need for that, gentlemen. I was only about to take my seat. I did book the table, after all.'

'Your gloves – remove them at once,' snarled Holmes.

'Forgive my bundled-up appearance. The fog affects my circulation. I am something of a valetudinarian and my aversion to this chilly, damp climate of ours inhibits me taking off my gloves, except in more comfortable, humid conditions such as a palm house.'

'Your gloves,' my colleague said impatiently, seizing the fellow's wrists with all his considerable strength, trying to prise off one of Sands's gloves, rolling the leather down the sleeve and causing a shriek of muffled protest.

'My apologies. My, these are a stiff fit, and quite a large pair, too.'

Despite a struggle, Holmes managed to unravel the pigskin leather and roll the stiff material down the wrist, exposing what should have been knuckles – what should have been a human hand.

There was a shocked, numb silence about the table. Only Doctor Wu took it all in his stride, stepping up behind his patient, appearing to slap Ethby Sands's overcoat pocket very hard for some inexplicable reason.

'Oh my God!' exclaimed Christopher Chymes.

'The bristling fur, those calcified yellow claws! What are you, Sands – man or beast?'

Taking full advantage of the outrage caused to his dining guests, the obvious repulsion towards his rare medical condition, Sands bounded across the room, flinging open the doors and leaving the Criterion to recover some of its respectability and panache.

'It is done, Mr Holmes. The end is near. Only a matter of time before Ethby Sands is no more,' said Doctor Wu.

'What on earth are you driving at, Doctor Wu?' asked my companion, settling back into his chair. 'What end are you talking about?'

'My dear sir, on the night of the theatre murder, after leaving yourself and Doctor Watson at Baker Street, I took it upon myself to seek out my wayward patient to form a proper diagnosis, this time to assess the likelihood that his acute medical condition had become untreatable. Sure enough, I and my team from the Mayfair clinic found him at home at Albany, sulky and uncooperative, his trusted companion, the valet Garson, out visiting Soho on his night off. He seemed lonely and agitated. I told him to lie upon the couch and I would administer acupuncture to lower his surfeit of Yin vacuity. I should do my best to calm the seven aspects, to settle him down for the night, to which he agreed. After he had drifted into a state of deep rest, my associates Chang Li and Fu Wung, who had accompanied me at short notice to Piccadilly, set into motion a plan I had held in reserve in case of emergency. Delicately un-stitching Ethby's Savile Row winter overcoat, a number of magnesium oxide strips and sachets of gunpowder were inserted between the coarse outer material, a tough tweed fabric. The silky inner lining of the garment had now gained some added padding but not noticeable to the wearer. A tiny strip of magnesium was stitched into the left-hand pocket, and now the overcoat becomes lethal. Add a tiny ampoule of sulphuric acid, placed in the bottom of the pocket, one merely has to break the phial to set off a chain reaction. The combustible material ignites, thus causing the extremity of the magnesium plate to dissolve to form a super-intensity of heat that melts anything and everything it makes contact with. Perhaps you noticed me, Doctor Watson, deliberately slapping the side of his pocket earlier?'

'In effect, he will become a human torch,' said Langton Lovell, tucking into his delicious lunch, pausing to sip champagne.

'Exactly.'

'Remarkable,' said I, 'but could you not have simply finished him off with an overdose of morphine, for example?'

'I do possess certain ethics, dear doctor. I am a practitioner of Chinese alternative medicine. No, I decided upon one last chance – one last opportunity to see whether I could cure my patient of this surge of aggression and bodily change.'

'But his metabolism is already so far infected,' I pointed out. 'The rat's genes have overwhelmed his system.'

'Indeed, Doctor Watson, but I undertook one last experiment. My intentions were wholly honourable, gentlemen. By a skilful combination of medical lancing and radical use of transfusing a main artery in his abdomen with a solution consisting of powdered rhinoceros horn and black bear claws, ling zhi, red ginseng, luo hau guo, and dried curled snake finely reduced, I proposed to cleanse his blood supply of impurities and purge the system, hopefully reducing the overwhelming presence of ratty antibodies.'

'You succeeded?'

'Alas, my efforts were thwarted, for Ethby Sands surprised us by waking from his deep state of rest. Upon realising he was about to have a medical procedure performed on him, that my team were stooped over him, eager to affix a length of rubber hose to his stomach with a long, sharp needle, he leapt up from the sofa and refused treatment.

'Pouring us all a glass of sherry, he said that he felt much better for his rest and would be going out for a short stroll along Piccadilly. My patient instructed me to gather you all together for luncheon at the Criterion today, at noon, where he would vehemently defend himself against allegations he was (a) a bounder and cad, and (b) he was a murderer. He then left, to my knowledge, Albany, heading out into the fog of Piccadilly.'

19

Calamity at the Statue of Eros

The Criterion is very close to the water fountain and statue of Eros, that decorative centrepiece so much sought after by tourists visiting the capital.

In ordinary circumstances, I should not have cared less for the sculpture of the archer and his bow for I had passed it hundreds of times in a cab or omnibus, but presently it was about to become marked as positively sepulchral!

We rushed outside just in time to witness a hansom pull out from beside the kerb, heading off in the direction of the Café Royale, the rows of fashionable arcades and Regency façades due east of the Circus. Suddenly, smoke began to billow out of the cab window and we heard a piercing, agonising howl, even above the clamour of omnibus and dray traffic.

'He is alight!' exclaimed our Oriental companion with minimal emotion, tall and noble, wearing his silk dragon robes and pill-box hat. 'Magnesium burns with an intense white flame. The metal strips inside the lining of his overcoat shall be activated, the ferromagnetic alloy set off by an acid concentrate released from the glass ampoule I deliberately smashed in his pocket. Next will come searing heat capable of melting human flesh. Need I say more, gentlemen?'

I recall a vivid, immense white flash, the force of the explosion overturning the cab, sending it careering across the road, mounting the kerb, before smashing into the fountain. The cab man and poor old nag I can report fatally injured. Neither man nor beast stood a chance.

Even as the wreckage burnt, worse was to follow, for Ethby Sands – or what he had become – was not dead, either from the smash or from magnesium melting his flesh like butter. Something inhuman, unrecognisable as a person, emerged from the rent and twisted remains of the burning coachwork. A sub-human torch clutching its fiery face, hair and clothes alight, struggling to gain purchase and climb up the statue of Eros, the archer and his bow at its pinnacle. It was not to be, for the fire had gained such hold that the heap of immolated rags lost its footing before the cremated remains fluttered down onto the pavement, collapsed in a blackened, charred husk.

I was aware of the urgent noise of clanging bells, for a fire-brigade pump was approaching from what I assumed was the direction of St James. Police whistles were much to the fore also, as crowds flocked along Piccadilly to find out what had happened. Carriage traffic had ground to a standstill. Joining other shocked pedestrians in the vicinity, we gathered round the statue of Eros, but none could get close to the burning carriage because of the intense heat. Bracing ourselves, we moved as close as safety would allow, beaten back by the flames licking hungrily at the base of the statue, showers of ash, sparks and trailing smoke rising into the air. The iron ring surrounding the spokes of one of the cab's wheels was still spinning, emanating a red glow, so hot had it become.

While Holmes and I were assessing the situation, an impudent fellow shrouded in a cloak and wearing a low-brimmed hat surged forward out of the ensuing commotion and tapped Christopher Chymes on the shoulder.

'Such a pity about old Garson, burnt to a crisp like that. My old valet rather enjoyed dressing up in my mohair overcoat and wearing those ridiculous "Joke shop" claws. He was a good mimic, you see, could imitate my voice and created a lasting impression – first-rate performance to be proud of, duping you all into believing it was I, Ethby Sands, who had barged into the Criterion restaurant. I shall explain everything at a time and place of my own choosing. I shall expect you gentlemen at Albany at four o'clock precisely. I promise to be contrite and apologetic regarding my recent unwarranted behaviour. Oh, and Doctor Wu Xing, on the last occasion we met I regret to say your so-called acupuncture treatment failed to induce the desired effect, placing me in a catatonic trance. In fact, I was feigning sleep, aware throughout, I saw and heard everything. Good day, gentlemen.'

20

Albany Revisited

We were in a grim and pensive mood when, on
that chilly late afternoon of a cold and dank
November day, we entered Albany's front entrance
and were shown upstairs to Sands's exclusive set
by a liveried porter who had been previously
advised of our impending visit.

Welcoming us, Sands, wearing polished red
loafers, tartan stockings, an exclusive green tweed
suit and a gold fob watch-chain in his waistcoat,
was charm itself, politely taking our hats, coats
and walking sticks, and ushering us into the sitting
room with its glass display cases full of stuffed red
birds of paradise.

There, above the mantelpiece, was the same gilt-
framed portrait in oils I had seen the last time I
was here. Ethby Sands, M.P., painted at the House
of Commons. By his careworn expression, heavy
jowls, pouches beneath the eyes, grey hair and
grizzled side-whiskers, and the wrinkled folds of
skin about his scrawny neck, I should have placed
his age in the portrait at pushing on eight and fifty,
and yet here he was unsettlingly in the flesh, stood
over by the Chinese Chippendale chair, looking at
most twenty-one years old. I confess it was hard to
fathom we were in the presence of a monster who
had already cold-bloodedly killed three people,

two of them in Norfolk, and who by usage of a controversial serum was enabled to stay young and active, staving off the effects of ageing and ultimately his own death from a wasting disease.

'This just can't continue,' said Doctor Wu, ever noble and calm in a crisis, this in the face of a dangerously volatile patient who could at any time change into a violent, rabid animal. 'Come to my Mayfair clinic. I can offer you renewed detoxification. We can at least stabilise your condition and prevent further unfortunate mishaps occurring. Surely you have had your fill of revenge. Philip Troy, for instance?' His eyes twinkled with perception.

'My physician speaks both eloquently and wisely,' remarked Ethby Sands, lighting an Egyptian cigarette. 'Gentlemen, help yourselves to whisky and splash, we shall toast my imminent demise. I shall myself abstain from alcohol.'

'You mean...?'

'I mean *our* imminent demise, Mr Holmes, for you and your compatriots here are about to join me in a final, wondrous climax to my life and work. Regard if you will the japanned upright piano over in the bay, on which I composed a popular hymn, still in vogue after all these years. Thirty million copies of sheet music sold and still counting. After Dr Wu Xing and his medical team had departed Albany for Mayfair, and with my valet Garson still out late on his night off visiting one of his lady friends in the vicinity of Soho, I conceived of a means of destruction even more spellbinding and futuristic than Doctor Wu's lethal winter overcoat, which I am sure we

97

all applaud for its ingenuity.

'I myself have created this morning a lethal piano, and here's how it works. You will each of you in turn step forward and play a white or black note of your choosing on the keyboard. We, gentlemen, are about to embark upon a game of "musical Russian roulette", because one of the notes on my little piano, when struck, will accordingly blow us all to kingdom come and destroy Albany forever, together with my other esteemed residents who share this most prestigious of London addresses. My piano keys are basically linked to several bundles of dynamite. I shall not give too much away, lest our sleuth-hound Mr Holmes using that damn clever brain of his outwits its workings. I think you'll agree I've not been idle. If you fail to come forward and take your turn I shall shoot you point-blank, blow each of your brains out with this pair of sophisticated silver repeater pistols I purchased from Naysmith of St James earlier. Are we all clear?'

'Perfectly so,' remarked Holmes 'May I smoke?'

'Of course, I shall allow a ten-minute interval before we begin – enough time I'm sure to concentrate your minds and prepare for your imminent demise – just as I had to do when I was languishing in my wheeled chair when those Harley Street doctors had given me but a fortnight to live. Alas, I must report one day the serum Doctor Wu developed in Norfolk will become depleted and I shall feel all the effects of accelerating old age and bodily collapse and sickness, which I am loath to endure, the wasting disease returning with a vengeance. No shaman or potion will be able to protect me from that, I can assure you. Why, Chymes, you will be first to play a note on my piano. I see you're trembling already. This only increases my enjoyment of the proceedings.'

'One moment if I may, Sands. Might I clear up a few points?' Holmes asked, puffing on his pipe.

'Of course, Mr Holmes. I should be glad to answer any questions you may have. But only eight and a half minutes remain, so be brief.'

'What part did your valet Garson play in all this?'

'Why, Mr Holmes, let us hear your own deductions, your brilliant mind must have surely formed its own conclusions by now.'

'Very well – my personal view is that it was he who was ideally situated to administer the alkaloid poison. By what means is unclear, whether with your meals or night-time drink, I'm not sure. Be that as it may, Chymes and Troy, both of whom wished to speed up your death so they would avoid lengthy and expensive litigation and the adverse publicity caused should you have gone to law over their blatantly plagiarising your original ideas for the musical, wished to recruit your valet and let him in on their dastardly scheme.'

'You are correct. Garson chose to betray me,' admitted Ethby Sands indignantly. 'He was impatient, you see. Like them, he wanted me out of the way, but for a different reason. With me dead he would benefit financially from a generous settlement in my will. I suppose you, Chymes, and your partner in crime Philip Troy, paid him handsomely for his trouble. But of course your scheme was doomed from the moment I decided to embrace alternative medicine and, as a last resort, visit the Mayfair clinic of Dr Wu Xing. It was he who, during my course of detoxification, informed me that apart from the wasting disease, my blood contained traces of a powerful alkaloid. But Garson paid for his duplicity in the end. The fool knew nothing about the lethal overcoat and loved dressing up and impressing people. I bet him a substantial sum that he would not be able to impersonate me and penetrate the luncheon at the Criterion. Of course, I was double-crossing him, for I was well aware of Doctor Wu's intention to eliminate me at the earliest opportunity.'

'What was your valet's view of the controversial serum?'

'Naturally, Garson witnessed for himself the miraculous transformation brought about by the serum developed by Doctor Wu and his team of microscopic chemists in the privacy of Norfolk, the undisputed fact that after a course of injections, I, a middle-aged man, had become young again after spending virtually a year as a crotchety old invalid, and was able one morning to simply get up from my wheeled chair and walk out of the door. Why, instantly he rejected Chymes's and Troy's plan to kill me and must have decided I was worth more to him alive than dead. Now I was in good health, more like my old self, our companionship flourished. But, as you now know I never forgave his duplicity – never.

'Dear me, we only have a couple of minutes remaining. A glass of lemon bitters, if you please Doctor Wu. I am all of a sudden grown weary of this conversation.'

'Allow me,' said Holmes, stepping behind me and pouring from a carafe.

'Drink it all down, Sands,' said the Oriental physician kindly, giving his patient a confident stare. 'Your blood sugars must be low. The lemon bitters will refresh you, the quinine perk you up a bit.'

'Yes, a tonic is all I require,' he agreed, taking the glass from Holmes and draining it before placing it upon the sideboard. 'Doctor Wu Xing,' said he with a sudden rush of passion, 'I owe you so much. Despite everything that has happened I shall always value our friendship, our doctor-patient relationship has endured. Please allow me to extend my...'

'What the!' The Chinaman looked on in astonishment as Ethby Sands quite unexpectedly was seized by an apoplectic fit, pitching forward, his eyes bulging out of his head, before landing plump at our feet, quite dead. Sprawled on the luxurious Turkey rug he lay perfectly still, very much the corpse, aptly surrounded by glass-fronted cabinets containing his stuffed collection. His beloved japanned upright piano mercifully remained untested, the lid firmly closed upon the keys by Christopher Chymes. At last we could breathe a sigh of relief. The exclusive Albany would not be obliterated in a frightful explosion and, thank heavens, neither would its inhabitants. Chymes was unable to bear the sight of the body, mortified by its presence, so we adjourned to the master bedroom and shut the door firmly behind us.

'Cyanide is a remarkably swift-acting poison,'

my illustrious colleague remarked, striking a match to his ever-present pipe. 'While Doctor Watson obscured me from view, I was able to empty a pharmacy bottle into the carafe. One always prefers to come to these types of meetings prepared. We had better inform Lew Shadwell, the porter downstairs, to put out an urgent request for an undertaker. We shall of course require a death certificate, which Watson thoughtfully brought along in his wallet. Doctor Wu, you will please act as witness to the signature.'

'I should be honoured,' he exclaimed, addressing my friend with a majestic bow, for the first time his thin, cruel lips breaking into the faintest smile. 'Although as a man of science, a practising physician, I should much prefer...'

'To retain his body for further analysis and research into your nefarious anti-ageing serum? I'm afraid, Doctor Wu, that would be out of the question. Might I further enquire about a compostable lightweight coffin, a wickerwork shell casually observed in the billiard room at Foxbury Hall at the end of October? Placed on top of the billiard table, I believe it was.'

'I normally use these for conveying difficult patients who I first, by means of acupuncture, induce into a state of deep rest and when subdued place in the shell. We can generally move a patient from A to B like this very effectively. Once more, my Mayfair clinic's superior advances in patient care come to the fore, Mr Holmes.'

'So this is presumably how Mr Sands was removed from Foxbury Hall and travelled down to London?'

'Exactly. He remained very composed, lying comfortably in the guard's van for the duration.'

The conversation was suddenly interrupted by a very worried Christopher Chymes tapping Holmes on the shoulder.

'The body's gone! I only went into the bathroom to splash water on my face – I tell you it's completely disappeared!'

We rushed into the sitting room and all stared dumbly at the space on the Turkey rug where Ethby Sands should have been lying dead ... but wasn't.

21

Mr Shadwell Returns

The autumnal gales and spell of wet and windy weather in London were succeeded by a static, impenetrable pea-souper. The dun-coloured fog blanketed the capital, refusing to budge for days on end, making travelling outdoors unpredictable, many of us preferring, unless absolutely necessary, to stay closeted indoors by our fires. At least our chimney had ceased to smoke and we were no longer susceptible to sudden gusts of wind dislodging soot into our grate, causing a mild panic.

'The new musical at the Wimborne has been feted by the critics as "an unstoppable success",' said I, turning over the pages of my *Daily Telegraph* while Mrs Hudson cleared away the breakfast things. My companion merely assented.

'Lovell and Lemon must be over the moon,' he answered, 'and Broadway beckons, I hear. To have achieved a guaranteed move to New York in such a short space of time is extraordinary. I suppose Christopher Chymes must be lapping up the adulation.'

'And raking in the really big money.'

'Certainly.'

'And nothing has been heard or seen of mutated old Sands – thank God.'

'If Doctor Wu Xing's prognosis is to be believed, he is of the opinion – and he backs this up with scientific testimony – that like many animals, particularly rodents, Ethby Sands has, in all probability, skulked off to die in some dark corner, cleaving to the shadows. A nest in a Metropolitan Line underground tunnel, or a remote alley, or an old, unused warehouse. The cyanide dose, Watson, was significant. It could have killed an elephant! Granted, Wu makes the point that Sands's rejuvenated system could have been resistant to the poison, showing only initial heart and respiratory collapse before recovering enough to escape Albany, but, really old man, that is just too far fetched.'

'Is it?' I shrugged.

'Well, let's hope...'

A knock at the door to our rooms heralded the rather faltering, hesitant figure of Lew Shadwell, as before, bowler held penitently in hand as though we might be about to reprimand him over some paltry misdemeanour – filching tuck-shop money, selling postcards to tourists at overly-inflated prices. He made his appearance once more wearing those maroon trousers with the distinctive emerald green strip running down the side, marking him out straightaway as a house porter at prestigious Albany – one of the finest addresses in the West End.

'Lo! I has a very urgent and unpleasant matter to inform you about, Mr Holmes. I h'am frantic with worry and beg you'se and Doctor Watson to accompany myself back to Piccadilly this instant.'

'My dear fellow!' exclaimed Holmes, rushing forward to assist our visitor. 'Come closer to the hearth. Watson, a stiff brandy – hurry, for Mr Shadwell is on the precipice of utter collapse. What is it man? What the deuce causes you to look so pale and distressed?'

'Blood.'

'Great heavens, not that blasted Cherry Blossom shoe polish again,' I gently chided the porter in an ill-conceived attempt to lighten the mood.

'I'se certain this time, gentlemen. Blood h'it is. Blood. H'it was the high-class milliner in No. 38 what alerted me to his ceiling, like. "It ain't bathwater, is it? Overflow?" says I. Well, Gryce Wharton is almost royalty – he designs elegant hats for Her Majesty, turns out all manner of flamboyant creations for aristocratic ladies – European princesses amongst 'em – I mean, Wharton's of Bond Street is an institution. Mr Wharton has occupied a set at Albany for close on twenty years, and I never once heard a word of complaint or 'ad any bother concerning noise or rowdiness. Like all our residents, 'e is a confirmed bachelor who keeps himself to himself and demands complete privacy. Correctly so, in my opinion, for 'e is a gentleman most proper and upstanding.'

'Here, drink your brandy Mr Shadwell. You are amongst friends – you have my complete attention.'

Leaning forward in the fireside chair, the porter held his head in his hands and openly wept.

'I'se just can't bring myself to do it – open that bleedin' door. No matter how much I tried I was froze. I was trembling so much I couldn't even hold the key straight. And downstairs on the landing Mr Wharton hysterical – sobbing like me now, clinging to 'is assistant Frederick like 'is life depended on it. You've gotta come to Albany right away, Mr Holmes, there's blood dripping from the ceiling in Mr Wharton's bedroom.'

'Who lives upstairs? Whose door can't you bear to open, Shadwell? Who is it residing in the apartment directly above Gryce Wharton? Come on man, out with it.'

'Mr Christopher Chymes, sir.'

22

Bloodbath

Holmes and myself have long been acquainted with pathology and human anatomy. After all, I am a trained doctor who saw service in Afghanistan, and he a consulting detective. Mr Shadwell, a decent, caring sort, was also in his profession used to dealing with crises. Even so the horror of the murder scene proved too much for the poor fellow to stomach and he quite properly left us to it, fully resigned that for the first time in its long and illustrious history, Albany should play host to a fully-fledged murder inquiry instigated by none other than Inspector Lestrade of Scotland Yard. I promised Holmes not to irritate readers by 'sensationalising' certain forensic details. The minutiae of examination of the scene by police officers can be found on file (incidentally, the case remains unsolved), but I shall instead relate that the composer appeared to have been caught unawares, asleep in the master bedroom, and that he was clawed to pieces and his body parts distributed around the flat.

'So, Ethby Sands was definitely shamming, then,' said I, as our cab trotted along Piccadilly, bell tinkling, carriage lamps dimly aglow. 'The cyanide had little effect.'

'By Jove, that appears to be the case, my dear Watson. I think, for diversion, despite this fog, we shall seek out St James's Hall, for there is a first-rate recital of Mozart's Overture to *The Magic Flute* starting in half an hour.'

23

Letter from New York

The Giant Rats of Sumatra was enjoying its season on Broadway to great acclaim, the London production coming to the end of a highly success-ful run. It is certain the murders of its composer Christopher Chymes and lyricist Philip Troy, generated a huge wealth of interest amongst mem-bers of the public, but it would be on the whole wrong to judge the success of the light opera solely on the grounds of morbid publicity, for many of the tunes were first-rate and audiences both here and in America flocked in droves and applauded the stage presentation. The choreography, most importantly the show, appealed to all ages and a wide range of social classes. But, I digress.

Eighteen months had passed and I was married to the love of my life, Miss Mary Morstan. I had since established a modest practice in Padding-ton inherited from my predecessor, who had retired on the grounds of ill health.

One warm evening in July, it so happened that both of us were absent from home, walking out in Regent's Park and attending a bandstand concert given by the Royal Grenadiers. Our maid an-swered a summons to the front door of our modest terrace and, as she later put it, 'a tall chap, pale an' thin as a beanstalk with a big beaky nose what made 'im look like a vulture asked me to give you this, sir.'

Here, then, was a manila envelope addressed to me and bearing my dear friend's neat, copper-plate writing.

Mary was for an early bed, so I hurried to the privacy of my surgery and tore open the envelope. Lighting my pipe, I settled down behind my desk and perused the contents – a couple of pages, the top missive a letter from Ethby Sands in New York, the other a short printed article cut out from the *New York Times* and gummed on a piece of paper with an accompanying note in the margin by Holmes:

My Dear Holmes,
I am in New York for the Broadway production of the light opera The Giant Rats of Sumatra, *for which incidentally I do not receive a penny. This, despite the whole concept being an original idea of mine and the stirring 'Flight of the Birds of Paradise' overture my own composition. By the time you receive this letter, both Langton Lovell, the theatre impresario, and his business partner Charles Lemon, the actor will be dead – murdered in customary fashion. I am living in a warehouse district of New York harbour. At night I am unable to resist the lure of the water and go for long contemplative swims round the bay to the Statue of Liberty, wondering what fate holds in store for me.*
Yours ever, Ethby Sands

Extract from the New York Times

Mister Stacey Davidoff, Harbour Master, only

confirmed what Captain Szyliowicz of the N.Y.P.D. had told the press earlier. The propeller of a New York harbour steam ferry became fouled up yesterday evening, causing the vessel to partly capsize. Nobody was injured and the passengers were all accounted for. Using a searchlight, it was determined that a rodent of unusual size had become tangled with the propeller after swimming out into the bay. New Yorkers are amazed that large vermin are allowed to flourish and, presumably, proliferate in the vicinity of the harbour. Sanitation Officer Stephen Bonetti assured the public that similar to the ongoing argument over giant alligators inhabiting New York sewers, a giant rat is nothing more than a myth.

Note: Both Langton and Lemon, then in New York, were unaware that any attempt was to be made on their life, and it appears Ethby Sands died before he was able to implement his plan to murder the impresario and actor respectively.
S.H.

The publishers hope that this book has given you enjoyable reading. Large Print Books are especially designed to be as easy to see and hold as possible. If you wish a complete list of our books please ask at your local library or write directly to:

Magna Large Print Books
Magna House, Long Preston,
Skipton, North Yorkshire.
BD23 4ND

This Large Print Book for the partially sighted, who cannot read normal print, is published under the auspices of

THE ULVERSCROFT FOUNDATION